Through MY EYES

THE FIRST FIVE

BOOK ONE

A

Dimitri Valentene

NOVELLA

Dimitri Valentene

CONTENT WARNING!

This book contains scenes that reference:

Age Gap

Explicit Sexual Content

FFMM

Gangbang

Mild Violence

Sexual Abuse

Suicide

All characters portrayed in this novella are fictitious and over the age of 18. Any similarities to real persons living or dead are coincidental and not intended by the author. To the extent, any real names of individuals, locations, or organizations that are used in the book, are used fictitiously and not intended to be taken otherwise.

Dimitri Valentene

Through My Eyes – The First Five

Table Of Contents

Dimitri Valentene

Through My Eyes – The First Five

Prologue

My name is Darion Valentine. At eight years old, I was involved in a brutal car accident where I suffered several broken bones, head trauma and was bedridden for nearly a year. The four years after comprised of bi-weekly check-ups, multiple medications a day, minor physical therapy sessions every Tuesday and Friday, and copious amounts of affection from my parents.

Fully recovered, I was different—something inside of me changed. With a single touch, I saw into people's minds.

The first time it happened, I was terrified— I thought my brain was broken. I dove into my dad's mind and what I saw was far from pleasant. I realized then that

I had free, unrestricted access to every single memory a person had. I could see everything they ever thought about, every decision they ever made, every idea that crossed their mind…and every erotic fantasy they concocted and experienced.

By the time I turned eighteen, I had a fair handle over my abilities. Learning control by regularly using it on my parents, they were always surprised when I knew exactly where all the Christmas gifts, birthday presents, and snacks were hidden.

Admittingly growing up, I used it more than a few times to get my way and quickly learned of the consequences. Whenever I abused my abilities, I would get these horrible nightmares and be haunted by some of the strong emotions from my parents' memories. After my first nightmare, I was terrified enough to tell them. If I was ever going to manage my abilities, I would need to talk about it and I knew my parents would listen.

Agreeing that it was best kept a secret, my parents made me vow never to use it on people without their permission.

It was a secret—I couldn't ask their permission…so in other words, don't use your powers.

At least that was how I tried to live my life, but Temptation is a seductive mistress…and who was I to refuse her demands.

Chapter One
High School Heat

With hands handcuffed behind her back, Miss Aly was completely naked on her knees in a bedroom. Her perfectly sculpted breasts and stiff nipples hung glazed with oil as she sat and patiently waited. Stepping out of the bathroom, her husband's voice pierced the silence.

"Are you ready for me, you little slut!?"

My dive into the pleasurable sensations of the flesh began with a teacher—Miss Alysandra.

Miss Alysandra was one of three Math teachers at my school. Solely tending to the upper forms, I was lucky enough to have her teach me math in form five. Miss Aly was not your average teacher, she often went the extra mile or ten for her students—the ones that made an honest effort in her classes, that is. As for the delinquents that often tried to disrupt her lessons, she never spared them her tongue and intentionally embarrassing scoldings. She was capable of being extremely cruel, yet once you were on her good side, she near adored you. Luckily for me, I was always good in math. Older than the rest of my classmates, I turned eighteen over the August vacation. It was no secret amongst my friends I had been held back a few times in primary school, but they rarely made fun of me. After all, I was the only student with a car…and my friends hated traveling.

I tried every day to park next to Miss Alysandra—it provided the opportunity to say goodbye every evening. All the boys and male teachers had eyes for Miss Aly. It was no surprise—she was breathtakingly beautiful. No taller than five feet and four inches, her petite frame was adorned by a prominent bust and a pair of curvaceous legs. Fancying pantsuits, her daily outfits highlighted her exquisite sandglass figure. A minimalist in terms of makeup, all Miss Aly wore was a brilliant shade of ruby red lipstick that accentuated her rich, caramel-coloured skin. Being the centre of attention in the staff room, it was no secret how other female teachers felt about her. They often made their issues with her known to students, playing it off as a slip of the tongue during classes. Despite all the attention Miss Aly gathered, she was always unphased—after all, she was a married woman.

In the middle of the first school term, form five students were given practice tests in place of mid-term exams in preparation for C.X.C. I had a single day of peace between exams—it was Wednesday, and I had sat through my math paper the day prior. Looking to ease the worries of my mind, I decided to meet up with some friends that were headed to a mid-day fete. Drinks, music, dancing, and women—exactly what the doctor recommended for what ailed me.

Meeting my friends there, I was greeted with the drunk chorus of, "Ohhhhh look who! You finally reach boy!"

Wasting little time, I delved straight into the festivities downing drink after drink. Nearing the evening, the sun crawled into the ocean and a once brightly lit sky faded to a blanket of black with scattered stars.

Standing amidst the crowd, with a drink in the air and her hips sensually swaying to the sweet Soca music was none other than Miss Alysandra. My feeble attempts to avoid her gaze made it a bit more obvious while my paranoid glances in her direction drew her attention, prompting her to make her way over.

"Darion, didn't you have school today?" was the first thing she asked in an attempt to break the ice.

"I could ask you the same thing Miss Aly." I tried keeping my cool so I said it as nonchalantly as I could.

"Touché Mr. Valentine, I guess we both decided to ditch."

Through My Eyes – The First Five

After a few awkward moments of sipped drinks and partial smiles, I ask, "You here alone Miss Aly? Where's your husband?"

Bringing an instant change to her mood, her face saddened followed by a deep sigh, "I'd rather not talk about my husband right now. Leave it at that."

Offering her a drink, we wandered off from the massive crowd of spilled alcohol and sweaty bodies. Indulging in polite conversation, we shared a few laughs and way too many drinks.

"Wanna dance?"

Her question rendered me speechless. My heart raced and my mind played its fantasies while my head nodded uncontrollably like an eager child that had just been offered a piece of chocolate. Flattered by my visible nervousness, she smiled and grabbed my hand, pulling me into the crowd. As we swayed to the music, my gaze often fell further south than I wanted it to. In a blue crop top, Miss Aly's cleavage was on full display, glistening with the sweat of a sweet Trini fete.

Catching me more than a couple of times, she turned around. Punishment for my wandering eyes I thought, but I was delightfully wrong. Leaning forward, she pushed back into me, burying my dick into the soft supple flesh of her perfectly shaped ass. Swallowing hard, I did my best to match her rhythm. Most of the time, I was completely mesmerized by the way Miss Aly moved—her grinding hips, flailing hair, and the ways in which she would sensually touch herself while grooving to the music—it was a bit much for my teenage hormones.

As thoughts raced through my head, playing erotic fantasies on a reel, coupled with my teacher's ass pressing firmly into my crotch, I felt that growing sensation. Going into a partial panic, I attempted to derail my mind, thinking about anything to avoid the awkward situation that had begun to erect itself. Each time Miss Aly pushed back, it got worse. Soon it was undeniable— fully erect, my cock sat comfortably between her cheeks. Not wanting to be embarrassed, yet not wanting the dance to end, I was stuck between a rock and a hard place.

Lost in thought, I failed to notice when she slowed her hips. Turning to me, she glanced down, lifting an eyebrow at the sight of my bulge. With little explanation, she leaned in and kissed me, cupping it with her hand. I'm not sure if it was my anxiety, the mass amounts of alcohol I had ingested, or both, but I accidentally saw into her mind.

With hands handcuffed behind her back, Miss Aly was completely naked on her knees in a bedroom. Her perfectly sculpted breasts and stiff nipples hung, glazed with oil as she sat and patiently waited. Stepping out of the bathroom, her husband's voice pierced the silence.

"Are you ready for me, you little slut!?"

With a fiery yearning consuming her body, the look in her eyes screamed, "Take me like the whore I am."

I was...

At that moment I had no idea how I felt—she was my teacher, and I was looking at her as she begged to be pleasured.

Standing in front of her, his thick, partially erect cock bobbed between his legs. Looking up with her bright brown eyes, Miss Aly opened her mouth and stuck out her tongue. With the head of his stiff dick, he traced her lips, smearing her ruby lipstick. Wrapping her lips around the tip, she flicked and teased him with her tongue. Deep breaths turned to audible moans as her husband rocked his head back while she sucked and worked his cock with her eager mouth.

Placing one of his palms on top of her head, he forced more of his veiny shaft into her welcoming throat.

"That's it, take it like a good whore."

Slowly moving back and forth, he slid more of himself into her. A ring of saliva formed around her lips as stringy drops made their way to her breasts and thighs. Slurping her husband's cock, she sucked faster and harder making that popping sound every time it slipped out. Cupping her face, her husband looked into her eyes before grabbing handfuls of her hair and ramming his eight-inch cock into her tight throat.

"Just like that… I love it when you struggle."

He held her face buried into his hips. While she fought, he tightened his grip and moaned louder.

"Yeah baby, just a bit longer."

Managing to break free from his grip, strings of saliva stretched from her lips—she coughed and gagged. Not allowing her the chance to catch her breath, her husband forced his cock back into her mouth and fucked her beautiful face furiously. Though she struggled and choked, she willingly let him have his way as her wrists fought against her restraints. In a matter of seconds, his penis was a blur flying in and out of my teacher's mouth as she gagged, coughed, and dribbled.

With watery eyes, she looked up at her husband enjoying every inch of her throat. His pace quickened and his thrusts became more forceful. His knees buckled, shoving it all into Miss Aly's mouth, her face was pressed firmly into his body, with her eyes growing wider.

"Fuck…I gonna cum!"

With growing moans, he held her head in place shooting streams of cum down her throat. Unable to breathe, she pushed him back causing him to spray lines of sticky white semen all over her face.

Snapping back to reality, my lips were still locked with Miss Aly's. Unable to properly process all that I had just seen, I stopped. Lost for words, I stared at her in silence for a moment or two before walking away.

Jumping into my car, I drove home and dreaded seeing her the next day at school.

That night, my thoughts kept me up. I kept seeing Miss Aly on her knees sucking her husband off, taking loads of cum on her face and in her mouth. Unable to help myself, I came five times that night. Each orgasm being more intense than the last. They never satisfied— instead, they always left me wanting more…more of her. Calling Miss Alysandra's name as I stroked my dick, I came again and again and again, into the wee hours of the morning. My lewd thoughts triggered a train of hormone-fuelled ideas—I had to see more of her. A single touch would have given me all I needed, but after that fete, I had no idea if she would ever speak to me again.

Chapter Two

The next day, I intentionally arrived at school late. Doing my best to stay out of sight, I avoided all the usual places Miss Alysandra would patrol. I was conflicted...I wanted to see more of her, but invading her mind seemed so wrong.

In the process of showering myself with guilt, I thought about how nice of a teacher she was. I recalled the countless times when she was kind and caring to me and many other students. Yes, she was a bit harsh at times, but that failed in comparison to the tenderness of her heart. I felt worse the more I thought about it, but then, for a moment, the image of Miss Aly on her knees with cum all over her face flashed in my mind. Reeled in by my fantasies, I heard her gag and slurp, I saw her eyes water as she choked on her husband's cock and moaned while licking the cum off the sides of her lips.

"Stop! She is your teacher and invading her mind is a nasty thing to do!"

Scolding myself mentally, I decided it was best to avoid her and wait out the rest of the term. Even though I still had scheduled classes with her—once I avoided any chance encounters, I would be spared the awkward situation and temptation—for today at least.

Lunch was over and I was still in the clear. With only a couple hours left before the final bell, it was not long before I could drive home. Enduring my final two classes, I frequently glanced at the clock in the classroom. With fifteen minutes left, the ease of relief began to set in and by the five-minute mark, my bag was packed and I was at the edge of my seat awaiting the bell. Three knocks rattled the metal door of our classroom. Opening it, our English teacher was greeted by Miss Alysandra. Peeking into the class, she pointed at me and demanded, "Mr. Valentine, I would like to see you after the bell rings. Meet me by the staffroom."

Immediately I felt nervous. Sitting in a rather cool air-conditioned classroom, I was warm...hot even, as beads of sweat rolled off my forehead. The, "Ooooooo," of my classmates did not help my anxiety.

The bell rang—it rang in my head all the way to the staff room, with it finally stopping when Miss Aly asked me to carry her papers.

Guiding me back to my now empty class, she made me sit and listen as she scolded me over my poor results from our last exam. In all honesty, the paper was easy, I just did not care for it as much seeing that it did not count towards our final grade; it was merely practice. Offering me her expert guidance through the paper, she insisted I stayed back and redo the entire thing. With little choice, I sat opposite her desk while she marked the rest of her tests. The silence was deafening, and the wild thoughts that danced in my head made it impossible to concentrate.

I had no idea why I said what I said—I summed it up to bad teen decisions, but before I could stop myself, the words were already past my lips.

"I'm sorry I left Miss Aly. When you kissed me, I knew you had a husband. It just…didn't feel right. Not that the kiss was bad, it was amazing, perfect even. Not that it was perfect kissing my teacher…well it was… it's just…"

Glaring at me mindlessly rambling, her face wore a teacher's sternness that rendered me a bit fear-stricken.

"Just complete your paper Darion."

Hearing the frustration in her voice I lowered my head. Feeling foolish, I did my best to concentrate on my exam.

When my mind eventually cooperated, and I was focused on my work, something brushed against my leg. Slowly inching upwards, it slid along the gap between my knees, rubbing my thighs as it found what it was looking for. Glancing down, I saw a stocking cladded foot gently rubbing against my crotch. Lifting my eyes, she was still buried in her papers, acting as if she was unaware of what she was doing.

I was lost in this situation…Do I sit and let her do what she wants? Should I undo my pants? Should I run? Ultimately, I was both unsure and eager at the same time, so I just sat there, trying my best to ignore it. The harder I tried, the more she moved her foot, rubbing and stroking along my stiff and throbbing cock through my pants. Waves of pleasure consumed me as I squirmed and shifted in my chair. All this time she acted as though nothing was happening. I felt my orgasm building, rising with each stroke. Through my heavy breathing, a moan ran past my lips, making her pause for just a moment. Her sudden stop prompted me to adjust myself causing me to accidentally push my pens off the table.

Removing her foot as I ducked under to pick them up, I was greeted by spreading legs. Inching her skirt up, she teased me knowing that I would have sneaked a peek. I swallowed hard senselessly gawking at her widening legs. Lifting my head out of sheer shock, I banged it under the table at the sight of her bare, freshly shaven pussy. Crawling back into my seat, I felt a wave of nervousness crash over me.

Keeping my head low, I avoided looking up at her as if my life depended on it. Seeing only my paper, I acted like I was deeply engrossed in my work. Soon a set of ruby, red-painted toenails appeared on either side of my test sheet. Trailing from her feet, up both curvaceous legs with my eyes, they ended at Miss Aly. Perched on the desk with her skirt pulled all the way up and her legs spread open, she looked at me with a lifted eyebrow. Balled up in her palm beside her were her pair of black panties. With a single finger, she instructed me to lean in, so I did. Once my head was in reach, she ran her fingers through my hair before tightening her grip and holding me in place. Her forcefulness had me stunned, so much so that I refused to resist.

Pulling my face into her warm slit, strings of her juices clung to her lips as they parted. I had no idea what to expect—I had never had oral sex before and all this was new territory. Sure, as a teen I often looked at porn, but this was completely different…this was real and happening right now.

With my face drawing closer, I had little idea what to expect and even less of an idea of what to do. I felt my mouth watering, but I had no idea why. I was so close that I could smell her. I had never smelled anything like her before—it was alluring, inducing primal urges as I revelled in its sweet intoxication. Opening my mouth, I felt the wetness of her pussy smear across my lips. Flicking my tongue slowly, I looked up as her breasts heaved under the weight of her breath. Leaning her head back, she held me in place as I licked and slurped her sweet nectar. Aimlessly working my tongue, I happened upon a spot that drove her crazy. Loving her reaction, I wrapped my lips around the soft flesh of her newly found clit, swirling and flicking it as waves of pleasure coursed through her body.

She grinded her hips into my face. Hooking both of her legs over my shoulders, she refused to release her grip on my head. Undoing her top, she unhooked her bra revealing her magnificent breasts. Fondling them with her hand, she circled and pinched at her pointed nipples. Her moans grew louder as random spasms riddled her body.

"Oh fuck yes! Make me cum, please make me cum!"

Not wanting to disappoint, I worked her hole until she orgasmed. Sliding my tongue into her wet, welcoming slit, I felt her insides pulse and tense up.

With a gasp, followed by a moan, her hips began writhing wildly under the guide of her trembling legs. Like a vise, she clamped my head with her thighs as her body twitched and spasmed. Warm liquid gushed out of her, running along my chin and dripping onto my uniform as her final moan eased beyond her lips.

I stared as her heaving breasts slowly steadied while her spasms eased, and her breathing calmed. Wiping her from my lips, she placed her feet against my chair, pushing me back as she hopped off her desk. With her skirt still pulled up, I admired her shapely legs and glistening pussy. Standing over me, we locked eyes. Her face was stern yet deceivingly suggestive—her stares screamed that she was in charge.

Not breaking eye contact, Miss Aly undid my belt. As my zipper slid down, its sound echoed in my head.

"This is really happening," I thought, convincing myself that I was here, awake, and it was all real.

In a swift motion, she slid my pants and boxers down. My bare ass now clung to the metal seat. Leaning in, Miss Aly threw her leg over me. With her eyes staring intently into mine, her stern expression was unphased as she lowered herself onto my stiff and willing cock. With a gasp escaping my lips as her wet slit kissed and parted at the head of my shaft, I was plunged into a sea of erotic sensations. With every inch that slid into her warm hole, a wave of ecstasy riddled my body.

Still locked in a battle of stares, Miss Aly dropped onto my lap, forcing my entire cock into her tight cunt. The metal chair dragged against the floor as it played one of the most erotic rhythms I had ever heard. Not taking it slow, she began riding me, bouncing up and down on my lap—my dick freely slid in and out as she got wetter. I felt her warmth between my thighs as her juices trailed down, dripping onto the chair.

With her hands on my shoulders, her pace quickened as the rattle of the dragging chair melded with the lewd sounds of slapping flesh and muffled moans. It was undeniable—I felt the fire in my loins as my orgasm encroached each time I slid into Miss Aly's tight, wet pussy.

"Fuck… I think I'm cumming"

Through My Eyes – The First Five

Whispered under her breath, it was the sexiest thing I had ever heard a teacher say. Her words were all it took. Moments away from erupting, I felt the walls of her pussy pulse. Her legs trembled, forcing her to lean into my body. Happily wedged between her tender breasts, she bounced her perfectly rounded ass until it was too much. No longer able to muffle our voices, we orgasmed in unison, filling the classroom with soulful moans of the flesh. With each pulse of my rod, I shot lines of cum into my teacher's sweet pussy as her insides tensed and relaxed under her climax.

After a few moments of gasping breaths, she stood up and fixed her skirt while gathering her papers. Before leaving the classroom, with me in it, she turned, "Go home Mr. Valentine, I'd regrade your test tonight."

I was beyond confused. Lost for words, I sat in silence for five minutes before making my way to the car park. On the drive home, I could still smell Miss Aly on my lips. Playing what had happened, over and over in my head, I failed to fight the urge to masturbate. It was risky, but I pulled onto the shoulder of the highway, parked, and pleasured myself to the thoughts, smell, feel, and taste of her. This was the beginning of my first sexual relationship.

Most school days, for the next couple months, Miss Aly and I would have sex after classes under the ruse of extra lessons. We rarely spoke, and during any meetings with her on campus, she avoided eye contact…but after school, she was different.

Dimitri Valentene

Once we had a classroom to ourselves, my body was all hers. She would grind her pussy on my face, ride my cock and make me tongue fuck her cunt until her body was contented. Personally, I had no complaints—our relationship was solely physical, and we never really spoke about our personal lives, especially her husband. The simple mention of him always put her in a bad mood.

Chapter Three

I was fucking my teacher. At least four out of five days for the week, she and I revelled in the sultry acts of forbidden pleasure. Keeping it a secret was a priority—I had no idea what the price was for fucking your student senseless in a classroom after hours was, but I am sure it was not one that Miss Aly could afford to pay. Though, sometimes, she walked that fine line between erotically exciting and reckless stupidity.

On occasion, the thrill that came from the chance of being caught made her pussy even wetter. Many times, during our escapades in risky locals around the school, I would slide her panties to her ankles, and they would already be soaked, with strings of her nectar slowly dripping off her mouth-watering slit.

27

In my entire life, I had only been in a couple of fights. As a lover, not a fighter, I refrained from violence—mainly because I feared getting my ass kicked. I did make a single exception during my high school years though. This guy was making a big scene with his friends, talking rather loudly about Miss Alysandra. Saying she dressed like a whore and what they would do if they had her. Before I could control the rage that flared in me, my fist was already flying through the air. In a heartbeat, it connected with his face as he fell to the ground. While his friends rushed to scoop him off the floor, someone shouted to us to get our asses to the principal's office.

Clearly being the one in wrong, according to the dean, the other boys were let off, while I remained pinned to a chair awaiting judgment. With my head in my palms, I contemplated what manner of scolding awaited me. While staring at the floor through my fingers, two sets of ruby-painted toenails came into view. Looking up I was met by a less than pleased Miss Alysandra posed with her hands on her hips and a pair of glaring eyes.

With no more than a finger, she made me follow as she guided me to her office. With me at her side, she strolled down the hallway with intent. The stern look that adorned her face made me fearful and admittingly a bit turned on.

All teachers had a small, private cubicle set on either side of the hallway, with a door on each—every teacher was allotted their privacy.

Through My Eyes – The First Five

Bursting into her office, I felt her frustration fill the room. Not closing the door all the way, I stood in the corner fidgeting with my fingers as she paced back and forth, reminding me that I was in a school, not a zoo. When she finally stood still, she glared at me from head to toe, and I could see the lust begin to foster in her eyes. Taking off her glasses, she placed them on her desk, near a stack of ungraded papers. Dragging out her chair, she pointed to the empty space beneath her table.

"Get under my desk and stay on your knees."

Her sharp and demanding tone made me fear questioning her, so I mindlessly complied. I ducked under her desk and dropped to my knees. I had a partial view of the bottom half of her entire office. I knelt, waited, and watched as Miss Aly slid her hands under her skirt, hooked her blue, laced panties, and slowly pulled them down. In a daze brought on by my pounding heart, I felt the blood from my body rush below my waist. As my dick pulsed, I felt the restriction of the fabric against my growing erection. I all but drooled, looking on as Miss Aly left her panties hanging off her ankle. Seeing her in high heels made my cock thicker and harder than it had ever been.

Lifting her skirt halfway up her toned thighs, she sat at the edge of her chair and rolled towards me. Nearing my face, her legs spread. Cornered by the metal sheeting at the back of the desk, I saw Miss Aly's hand come into view. Using her signature finger, she called me in and then pointed at her moist, dripping lips. Fully concealed under the metal table, I crawled forward on my hands and knees.

Her smell removed all reservations I had about the situation, and all I could think about was burying my face between her lips and tongue fucking her until I tasted her orgasm. Easing her legs over my shoulders, I pulled her in closer to the desk, tucking my head under her skirt. Having learned a thing or two from our many encounters, I employed all my prowess. Moistening my lips, I gently parted her with my fingers before kissing her clit. A single spasm rocked her entire body as the wheels of her chair complained with a sharp squeak. Dragging my tongue, I licked every inch of her wet lips and warm slit. My tongue fondly explored her pink flesh and her taste had long since bewitched my mind —I savoured every drop of her sweet honey but somehow it was never enough.

Leaning back into her chair, her heavy breathing turned to soft moans. Slapping her palm across her mouth, she bit into her finger as I felt her other hand weaving through my hair. Pushing her pussy harder into my face, her grinding hips made it difficult to breathe. Slow strokes were now small circles as the tip of my tongue played fondly with Miss Aly's clit. Drenching my chin and dripping onto the floor, her pussy drooled as she neared her orgasm.

"Miss Alysandra, what did you do with the student that was involved in the fight?"

His knocks against the door pushed it further open. Taking it as an invitation, the principal stepped in enquiring about me. Casually sitting up, she used her tight grip on my hair to pry me from between her legs. Strings of her erotic nectar clung to my lips as she pushed me away and held me in place.

"You can rest easy Mr. Mahabir, I dealt with him the best way I knew how. He should not be causing any more trouble, I assure you."

Her response promptly sent him on his way. As soon as the door closed, Miss Aly rocked back on her seat and yanked me towards her, slapping my face into her impatient cunt.

Having to work her up to a climax all over again was a great thing in my mind —it just meant that I got to have more of her. Parting her lips with my tongue, I teased her hole by barely sliding it in before sticking it as far up into her as it could reach. Wildly flicking and rolling my tongue, I felt the warmth of her insides as she gushed into my mouth. Taking me by surprise, she squirted, spraying my face, soaking my uniform, and ending with the echo of splashing water ringing through the entire office. Her legs trembled, gripping the arms of her chair as she attempted to tame the wild spasms of her hips. Astounded by what had just transpired, I whipped my face and licked her from my fingers.

Rolling her chair back, she tossed me a small hand towel. Cleaning myself up, I looked at Miss Aly, expecting her to say something, anything. Gript by the exhaustion of her orgasm, she groggily lifted her hand and pointed at the door, "Make sure no one sees you leaving my office."

Taking a breath to say something, I decided against it and quietly took my leave.

Our days of after-school sex carried on as I silently learned more and more ways of properly pleasing a woman. Nearing the final weeks of the semester, everyone at school scurried to prepare for the end-of-term sports day that was being held at the Ato Boldon Stadium. With the aura of chaos that loomed over the frantic teachers as they put everything in place, Miss Alysandra had little time for our sexcapades. For over a week, there were less than five words shared between us.

Unable to think straight, my nights were filled with porn and frequent masturbation. On repeat, I played each time I tasted and fucked Miss Aly in my head, bringing myself to some of the most intense orgasms I had ever experienced. Each time I came, I shot reams of cum wildly into the air while thrusting my hips. My vulgar thoughts often made me wonder about my feelings towards her. I had no idea as to whether I was in love, infatuated, or simply stricken by her erotic nature. With the ensuing anarchy in my mind, I decided to talk to her, hoping that she could at least offer some advice.

I thought it would be best to speak to her during the sports day—with the event going on I assumed she would have a little free time. Wanting to be a gentleman, I bought her a bar of chocolate from the many vendors that had set up shop for the event. I roamed the stadium for what felt like hours, perusing every row and scanning every corridor, but no one had any idea where Miss Aly was.

Through My Eyes – The First Five

The sunny skies turned grey and with a flash of lightning and the rattling boom of thunder, rain poured from the heavens. Drenching the field and all the students, few cared that they were getting wet while everyone else continued to enjoy the festivities. Giving up my search, I tagged along with a few friends who were headed to the car park. Having a secret bottle of rum concealed in a car they had rented; we all hid and shared a few strongly mixed drinks. Fearful of getting caught by patrolling teachers, I often scanned the carpark to ensure we were in the clear.

During one of my routine checks, I noticed that Miss Aly's car was parked some distance away from where we stood.

Both joy and anxiety flooded me as my feet pulled me towards her Mazda wagon. Squinting, I failed to see anything through her dark tint. The closer I got, the more nervous I became. My heart rammed rapidly against my chest but for some odd reason, I felt happy, as if I was doing the right thing. Soaked from head to toe, I made my way through the relentless rain. Mere meters from her car, I noticed it was slightly shifting from left to right. When I got closer and leaned in, I saw Miss Aly in all her naked glory, riding her husband's shaft as cum dripped from her pussy onto her leather seat. With his eyes shut feeling the aftershocks of his orgasm, her husband failed to notice me standing near the window, but Miss Aly did. Trailing some of the cum off her seat and onto her hand, she looked me dead in the eyes as she pinched her nipples and dragged her finger along her tongue. Though the

33

echo of battering rain rang loudly, I heard her sweet moan ringing in my head.

Shattered, I didn't even notice the chocolate had slipped from my fingers. Turning around, I felt an overwhelmingly sinking feeling in my stomach. With tears masked as raindrops, I sat on the massive staircase at the entrance and drowned myself in thought.

About thirty minutes later, Miss Aly dropped off in front of me before her husband drove off in her car. Shuffling to fix her clothes, she looked at me and for the first time I expected something other than the stern glare she often gave, but I was greatly disappointed.

I always thought she had hated her husband, but there she was, riding his massive cock in the car park while her students played games and ran races. With a sigh, she stepped towards me, not wanting to hear a word she had to say, I stood up and walked away. Behind me, I heard the clacking of her heels as she ran, before her firm grip took hold of my wrist. I was angry and heartbroken —without a proper hold on my emotions, it just happened…I dove into her mind. Seeing thoughts and memories of her husband, I realized that he was a good man. Working offshore on an oil rig, he was seldom around but did it to provide a good life for her. All this time, she was cheating on him, pulling me into her web of sex and lies.

Yanking my hand from her grip, I glared at her as tears ran from my face, "I loved you…you were my first!" I cried as I confessed.

Through My Eyes – The First Five

From the look on her face, I saw the flecks of guilt glimmer in her eyes, not knowing before that moment, that I was a virgin until her. Opening her mouth, I immediately thought about the manner of lies she was about to spit and before I knew it, I blurted out, "Stay the hell away from me or I'd let the entire faculty know you're screwing a student!"

Leaving her standing in the rain, I wiped my eyes as I walked away. Instantly regretting my remark, the sting of my pain justified my words, yet I felt greater sorrow knowing that I threatened her. After that day I tried my best to avoid Miss Aly and aside from questions during classes, she and I rarely spoke during my final two terms of high school. It was weird seeing your teacher at school, knowing that she was technically your ex-girlfriend. Needless to say, my last school year was not as great as it was when it had started. Miss Aly was my first—she had no idea until I let it slip, but I lost my virginity to her and the sultry times we shared were enough to get me through many lonely nights. Sadly, those memories were not as kind to my aching heart.

Chapter Four
The Gap Year

After graduation, I took a year off to figure out what I wanted to do with my life. Thinking back on it now, that year was the year my life changed the most. Freed from the prison that was my high school, I was glad not having to see Miss Alysandra again.

Considering enrolment in a local university, I had no idea what I wanted to pursue, and with the aches of my recovering heartbreak still plucking my strings, my thoughts were less than clear. My parents getting a divorce did not help, and seeing my old man go on more dates than me was like pouring salt into an open wound. Spending the first two months at home, life to me quickly got boring. Aside from a newly acquired taste for old motorcycles, I had nothing to show for my time away from academia.

Gathering the money I saved through the years of high school, I sold my car and bought an old Virago 400 from a man in Sangre Grande. Beyond happy to part with the motorcycle, he gave me all the spare parts he had, free of charge. With no money left, I got a job through a friend as a carpenter's aid—I did not make much, but it was enough to slowly restore my bike. Luckily with the help of YouTube videos and my dad's know-how, Gabriella was up and idling after a month. By pulling a few strings at the Licensing office, he ensured I got my motorcycle permit as quickly as possible and with his help, I bought a set of decent riding gear and took to the roads of Trinidad.

I was soon noticed—by posting pictures of Gabriella on social media, many cruiser bike groups invited me on rides and to the events they held. Before long, I had a massive group of friends, though none were better than Zatanni...kind and funny—the type that loved the thrill of the ride and sought adventure every chance he got. Dropping out of high school, he worked in construction to send his sister to school after his dad died. He was genuine and honest and was the only one there for me after my parents had gotten divorced. He was the first person that I ever spoke to about Miss Alysandra. His thoughts were that I was taken advantage of, but I knew deep down that was not the case.

As much as she used me, I enjoyed it. I welcomed it and relived those moments in my head as I masturbated and longed to smell her on my lips and taste her on my tongue again.

Usually, when our bike group did beach runs to Maracas, Zatanni and I would tag along for the chance to gawk at some beautiful custom motorcycles. On one particular ride, he was late for the first time and missed our usual meet-up at the Coffee shop. Failing to answer calls or reply to texts, I felt a bit discouraged about embarking on the impending group ride without him. Deciding to fly solo, in a lengthy line we trailed along the highway as our revving engines signalled our approach to nearby motorists. With the wave of bikers weaving through cars, kids pressed their faces against the glass of car doors to get a glance at the beastly machines. We left the highway, venturing onto roads surrounded by lush greenery and beautiful countryside.

In the chorus of growling engines, I heard one that was all too familiar. Pulling up alongside me was Zatanni. He hailed me with a salute through his helmet, his passenger perched behind him with her hands wrapped tightly around his waist. Adorned with a full set of black leather gear, the zipper on her jacket hung low enough to provide a clear view of her prominent cleavage. Pulling off, he darted to the front of the group as I was left bewildered, wondering who the hell was on the back of his bike.

One by one we all pulled up to the Maracas lookout, parking our motorcycles as random beachgoers stopped to take pictures and ask questions to the different riders. While sharing a conversation with an older gentleman who admired Gabriella, I saw her...

With her elbows pressed against the green rail, she stared out over the ocean as the sea breeze whipped the loosely wound curls of her sandy brown hair. The black leather of her jacket complimented her fair skin and emphasized her shapely legs, drawing eyes to the gap between her thighs. Leaning forward, she unknowingly swayed her ample, leather-cladded ass from side to side. Like a swinging coin, it hypnotized me, drawing me in like a helpless moth to a bug zapper.

In my senseless daze of walking up to her, I was apprehended by Zatanni. Throwing his arm over my shoulder, he insisted I meet someone. Pushing me towards the woman at the railing, my original destination, he plucked her attention from the amazing view.

"Darion, I'd like you to meet Ella... my little sister."

As she turned around, my eyes were drawn to her busty chest as her breasts struggled not to spill out of her fitted white crop top. From her navel hung a belly button ring—its silver metal and gleaming blue gemstones drew the eyes, pulling attention to her pink thongs clinging to either side of her hip.

I argued to myself as I leaned in for that awkward 'nice to meet you' hug.

"Surely this wasn't the sweet and innocent sister that Zatanni had spoken about..."

The little I saw of Ella's body was not enough. Indulging my urge to see more, I acted like a bit like an opportunist at that moment. Seizing the chance, I dove into her most private and heated thoughts. This was the first time I willingly invaded someone's mind.

Plunged into total darkness, soft gasps and shallow moans surrounded me. A rhythmic squeaking played in the background as voices chatted in between their utterances of pleasure.

"Fuck…. You're hugeee…mmhh!" A gentle voice moaned as the sound of slapping flesh grew to a furious pounding.

"I think I'm gonna cum!"

Her proclamation cut short when she gagged.

With a click, the lights sprung to life, reaching every corner of the room. I was in a university dorm, and on the bed to my left, Ella's naked body was wedged between three guys. Bent over, her back was arched while the rather muscular man behind her held her cheeks open as he rammed his rod forcefully into her stretching pussy. Her toes curled and legs quaked each time his hips slapped against her milky cheeks.

"Stretch my fucking pussy!" she begged through her gasps that came after each of his thrusts. Spanking her ass, he admired the sultry way her flesh rippled as he continued to work his long, meaty cock in and out of her dripping cunt.

With her pussy being pounded from behind, a skinny fellow—a friend of Mr. Muscular I presumed—gripped handfuls of her hair as he shoved inch after inch of his dick into her struggling throat. Fucking her relentlessly from both ends, she still managed to skilfully work a third shaft with her free hand, stroking and rubbing its oozing precum between her fingers.

I gawked as she worked three cocks while enduring one spasm-inducing orgasm after the next. She had wailed, "Fuck me harder, I'm cumming!" so many times, I lost count. With a sprawling grip that wrapped perfectly around Ella's waist, Mr. Muscular effortlessly lifted her so that her knees hovered slightly above the mattress. Driving his shaft as deep into her as her pussy allowed, he fucked her with a newfound ferocity.

Slapping echoes of flesh were overpowered by the sounds of her gushing hole as her juices spurted wildly from her stuffed pussy.

"Fuck yes!" Mr. Muscular proclaimed with pride. Her once shallow moans had erupted into screams of choked, climactic pleasure as she drooled profusely on the cock thrusting rapidly past her rounded lips. As she spilled at both ends, Mr. Muscular announced his approaching orgasm. Enduring a truly primal fucking for a few seconds, her hole milked every drop of cum from his pulsing dick.

Sliding out of her freshly fucked slit, his drooping cock was followed by a thick stream of white seed that dripped and pooled on the bedsheet.

"Mmmmhh…I love when you cum inside me," teasing as her ass swayed playfully from side to side. With her back still arched, she displayed her now gaping hole that gleamed with fresh cum as she worked her final two rods. Wasting little time, she stroked and sucked, eager for him to erupt and fill her mouth. With a thrust that buried all of himself down her throat, the skinny fellow proceeded to climax as his cock pulsed and shot lines of cum that dribbled past her lips and down his balls.

Taken by surprise, she flinched as her face was blasted by the orgasming cock between her fingers. Driven by her fiery urges, she opened her mouth to receive as the cum from her fresh face fucking still coated her tongue. With grunt-like moans, line after line of thick white semen shot from his pink head, draping along her face. Falling into the naked bodies of her lovers, she sighed a blissful moan before submitting to her exhaustion.

Yanked from her mind at the end of our hug, I snapped back to Zatanni scolding her. "Ella, pull up your pants and fix your jacket. Can't you dress like a proper woman?"

"Come on man, you of all people should know how hot leather motorcycle gear gets. Plus she's dressed better than half the biker dames here."

I interjected, attempting to be the knight in shining armor.

Earning me a smile, she blushed, hooking her hair behind her ear as I repaid her with a smile of my own. Glaring at me with a lifted eyebrow, Zatanni was less than thrilled at my bold attempt at flirting with his sister.

After buying a few refreshments from the many food stalls, the group mounted their bikes. Like a sweet symphony, the many machines roared in an ear rattling unison, echoing as we all rode along the winding roads to the bay. All the while, my mind was riddled with amorous flashes of Zatanni's sister—her dripping wet, gaping hole, her cum covered face, and the sweet serenity of her animalistic moans all urged an erection that made riding rather uncomfortable.

Chapter Five

Once at the beach, small crowds began forming around some of the bikes and their bikers. Though most of us enjoyed the attention, Ella was visibly restless and throwing a tantrum over the fact that she could not go into the water. After her many protests, each annoying Zatanni more than the last, I interjected yet again.

"Buddy, if it's okay with you, I don't mind going with her. I'd keep my eyes open, make sure she doesn't get washed out to sea and I'm a decent swimmer so if she does, I've got her covered."

Expecting to get punched or at least a harsh glance from Zatanni, both Ella and I were surprised when he just sent us on our way. I guess with an array of bikini-wrapped beauties asking him about his bike and to go for a ride, his sister was the last person on his mind.

Flinging a bag over her shoulder, she made her way to the changing rooms near the shoreline. After a few minutes of futile banging on the doors of occupied stalls, Ella grabbed me by the wrist and led us to a secluded place at the back of the changing rooms. Pulling a towel from her bag, she handed it to me.

"Here, hold this up for me."

Honouring her request, I held the towel open, draping it around her as the changing room wall provided extra cover from prying eyes. Zipping down her jacket, she revealed her white crop top. Removing her boots, she unbuttoned her pants, fully aware that I could still see her. Slipping it down past her butt cheeks, and over her ankles, she looked at me the entire time. My nervous swallow prompted her to giggle as she unhooked her bra. Turning my head, I averted my eyes, staring off into the plane of golden sand strewn with blindingly white beach chairs and umbrellas. Fighting the urge to peak, I fought my lewd thoughts and burning desire to see her naked body.

Feeling the growing excitement in my chest as my heart fluttered, I was pulled from thought by Ella's finger hooking my chin. Guiding my head, she pulled my gaze. Drawing attention to her glorious tits, she pressed them together as her perky, light brown nipples basked in the peaking rays of the island sun.

45

"If I didn't want you to look…I would have gone into one of the empty changing rooms."

Her words dropped me into an entirely new state of bewilderment. With widened eyes and a hanging jaw, Ella rendered me silent…a silence she used to clarify her earlier remark.

By turning her back to me, leaning forward, and slowly carrying her pink thongs to her ankles, she gave me a brief view of her voluptuous lips and bare cheeks. Tracing her hips with her fingers, she looked over her shoulder at me as a seductive smile drew across her face. Positioning her hands below her ass, she flicked her cheeks with her fingers. Biting her lips, she stared at my eyes as they were distracted by her jiggling flesh. Pulling her cheeks apart, a soft moan eased past her lips before she reached into her bag for her bikini.

"You okay there big boy?" she mocked as she brushed her hand against my tented shorts, gripping my cock through her towel. Thanks to her, I had to fidget with my erection before walking over to the water. Diving into the serene, sapphire blue of the refreshing ocean, we swam and splashed each other, exchanging friendly taunts and laughs.

Eventually, we struck up a conversation that mainly involved her talking and me listening. In some ways, Ella was a lot like Miss Alysandra—stern, demanding, and driven by a blazing urge of unrivalled sexual desire. Unlike her, Ella was a huge tease. She egged you on, drew you in, and made you crave her. She thrived on being desired and lusted over, yet she somehow convinced Zatanni that she was this innocent girl that could do no wrong.

As we spoke, the crashing waves played their rhythm while the seagulls sang overhead. In chest-high water, our toes fiddled with the sand beneath our feet as the lively ocean glistened under the Caribbean sun.

Already enrolled in a University, Ella was a year one psychology student at the University of the West Indies in St. Augustine. Having her own apartment near campus was a great convenience and worked perfectly for her lifestyle. With no prying eyes or adults hanging over her, she was free to do as she pleased, and whoever she pleased. With none to oppose her decisions, she explored all manners of her sexuality, a fact that she spoke openly about.

After chattering about school and basic stuff for half an hour, she shimmied through the water, making her way next to me. In a soft tone, she spoke as we locked eyes. Trailing my stomach, her hands made their way down into my shorts.

With slow strokes, she encouraged my erection as my cock slipped between her wandering fingers.

"You should hear me moan while getting my holes stuffed," she whispered.

Her words sent a rush to my cock as an odd sensation ensnared my senses. Listening intently, I spasmed and groaned between heavy breaths as she worked my hard rod beneath the water.

"Guys love to fuck my pretty face—they say my lips are to die for. Do you think so?"

Tracing her lips with the tip of her tongue, her fiery eyes had long since bent me to her will.

"Mhhh! I just love it when a man fills my mouth with his warm cum…I love it even more when they take their massive… veiny…thick cocks and stuff them into all three of my holes at once."

Pushing me over the edge, I struggled to mask my moans as I came. With each pulse of my dick between Ella's fingers, lines of cum spurted into the water.

While shaking off the aftershocks of my orgasm, we noticed Zatanni flailing his tattooed arms as he signalled to us that it was time to eat. Eagerly dashing towards the shore, Ella left me behind as I waited out the final moments of my receding erection, before venturing out to quell my hunger.

For the rest of the day, I was bombarded by Ella's frequent teasing—bending over slowly, giving me peaks at her nipples, and eating an ice cream cone in a way that could make the sun sweat. She boldly acted knowing her brother was always a stone throw away.

I knew it was wrong, but she hooked me in a way I had not felt since Miss Alysandra, and getting caught by Zatanni made it more exciting for us both.

Through My Eyes – The First Five

I could not go a solid fifteen minutes without Ella displaying herself to me—like a baited hook, her flashes were the bob of the lure and I a witless fish.

At the day's end, I had lost count of the number of erections I unwillingly had—my mind was flooded with countless, partial glimpses of Ella's magnificent body. Drained from an amazing day at the beach and desperately craving a release, I dragged my feet through the sand as I waded over to the changing rooms.

Stepping in, I noticed many of the stalls were occupied, but thankfully there was one available at the very end. Making my way over, I pushed the door open and placed the bag with my things on the concrete slab that jotted out of the wall. Latching the door behind me, I stripped down to my boxers and turned on the shower. Trailing my palms along my body, I did my best to wash off that dry yet sticky feeling the ocean water left on my skin. Startled, I nearly slipped at the sound of four knocks against my stall door.

"Hey, Darion, everywhere else is full. Mind sharing? Zatanni is in a rush to get going."

With silence as my answer, I stood with my hand on the latch, contemplating the repercussions of what I was about to do.

"Darion… are you going to let me in or not?"

She asked this time in a more serious tone.

Finding comfort in my silence, I cast all my reservations to the wind and unlatched the door.

Closing it behind her, Ella tossed her bag onto the concrete slab as I held my face beneath the icy droplets raining from the shower. From behind, I felt her arms wrap around my chest. Pressing her naked breasts against my back, the surprise sensation of our kissing flesh forced me to turn and face her. As the water flowed off our bodies, I tilted my head, staring with a lifted eyebrow at the landing strip, neatly trimmed along her mound.

Slowly taking to my knees, I guided one of her legs over my shoulder. Licking my lips, I inched forward, burring my open mouth into her eager slit. Parting the supple lips of her moist pussy, I slowly slid my tongue in and out of her hole, tasting her as she dripped off my chin.

After a few minutes, her legs trembled under the weight of her pleasure, forcing us to move over to the concrete slab. Pushing our bags aside, she placed her ass at the edge before hoisting her legs in the air and spreading them apart. Her display parted the lips of her pussy as the excitement slowly trickled from her hole.

Like a hooked fish, she reeled me in with a single finger. Mindlessly I rushed to drink her sweet nectar, sloppily eating her cunt until she had smeared every inch of my face.

Fishing in her bag, Ella let out a disheartening sigh, "Damn, I don't have any more condoms and I'm off the pill."

Her words cut like a blunt sword into the mood.

Beyond disappointed, I was urged to ask, "So what now?"

With a smile that suggested I was in for a treat, she bent over, placing one hand on the slab of concrete and digging in her bag with the other. Pulling out a small bottle of lube, she placed it upright, arched her back and peered over her shoulder before tapping her backdoor with her index finger.

Knowing fully well what she meant, seeing her tight little asshole on display fostered an unusual desire in me to try something new. Her head faced front while she patiently awaited the sensation of my cock prodding her ass.

With a gasp that did all but get us caught, she was taken by surprise as the warmth of my tongue brushed against her asshole. My face tucked proudly between her milky cheeks, my tongue flicked and poked as I made her feel something she had never felt, before rising to my feet and dropping my boxers.

Slathering my cock, I stroked it behind her until it was completely lubed. Covered with saliva, I dragged the head of my dick around the rim of her freshly licked ass. Applying little pressure, I felt myself slipping in. As she stretched to accommodate me, her shallow breaths grew to erotic whimpers that were drowned out by the busy showers. Feeling a ring of tightness, and pure bliss run the length of my shaft as I slid deeper into her, filled me with ecstasy. It didn't take long before every inch of me was buried deep in her warmth.

Placing my hands on her hips, I slowly moved back and forth, trying my best not to hurt her.

"I won't break Darion! Now fuck my ass like you realllyyy want it. Stretch my tight hole!"

Shocked by her demands, I was more than happy to comply. Tightening my grip on her slender waist, I rammed my cock into her now creamy ass.

"Fuck yes… Just like that… now make me cum!" she moaned.

Driven by a pure primal instinct, I relentlessly pounded away as her clapping cheeks echoed. Grabbing a handful of her sandy brown hair, I pulled her up, pressing her back against my chest as my dick slid freely in and out of her ass.

With her hair in hand, I pulled her head back, kissing her along her neck. Dragging my finger from her lips, I traced her nipples. Trailing along her flat stomach, I wandered over her mound and into her Netherlands.

Parting her wet lips with the tips of two fingers, I slowly worked them into her pussy while burying my shaft deep into her stretching asshole.

With lips against her neck, fingers working her drooling cunt, and a stiff rod up the ass, her orgasms were frequent, and her moans were loud. So loud in fact, that I was forced to hold my palm over her mouth so that other patrons of the changing room did not hear her orgasmic decrees.

Her muffled moans kept growing as her pussy gushed, again and again, rushing and trickling down her thighs. Falling under her quivering legs, I held her up as I continued to fuck her hungry butt.

Feeling the approach of sweet release, my thrusts into her became wild as my knees buckled. Going over the edge, I felt the eruption of warmth radiate through my entire body as my cock filled Ella's ass with every last drop of my cum.

After our duet of heavy breathing, we resumed our shower with some light kissing and left the changing rooms separately to avoid suspicion.

Seeing Zatanni in the distance when I walked out, I called him over, apologizing for keeping him waiting. Oddly, he had no idea what I had meant. According to him, the party was just getting started.

Overhearing our conversation, a passing Ella winked at me before displaying a sly, contented smile.

Dimitri Valentene

Chapter Six

After that splendiferous day at the beach, Ella and I saw more of each other while doing our best to keep Zatanni from finding out. We were not in a traditional relationship—an intensely physical one yes, but aside from me following her every command in the bedroom, we knew very little about each other.

Some nights I would stay at her apartment—never in a rush to have me leave, she always insisted I spent the night. Admittedly, after hours of sensuous passion, neither of us found the will to fight off our post-orgasmic fatigue. Falling asleep in near silence after our sinful yet satisfying ventures, Ella had a likeness for cuddling and remained in my arms most of the night.

Through My Eyes – The First Five

Though we often shared moments that could bring a man's heart to its knees, she made it quite clear that I was not the only man in her life. Openly she spoke about her adventures in the very bed we both slept in, sharing every intimate detail.

She often told me about her preferences, the positions that made her cum, the ones that made her squirt, and the fact that two cocks are indeed better than one.

I loved listening. When she spoke, telling me about the landslide of bliss her body experiences at the hands of other men, I could not help but become aroused. Her sultry tales only added to the rush and excitement, making for some mind-blowing sex afterward.

One night around one in the morning, while tucked into bed, my phone rang. In my sleep-riddled daze, I groggily rubbed my eyes as I brought it to my ear.

"Darion…," a sniffling voice whispered between sobs, "Could you come get me? I could really use someone right now."

Realizing it was Ella, I rose to my feet with urgency. Stumbling through my room, I tossed on bits and pieces of my gear while asking where she was. With a twenty-minute ride ahead of me, I thought it best to let my dad know I was going out.

Strolling down the hall, with my helmet in hand, I approached his door and prepared to knock. Halting my fist mere millimetres from his door, a horrific sound cursed my ears.

"Oh yeah, who's your daddy!?"

Nothing in the world could have prepared me for the sheer embarrassment of being able to answer the exact question that my father was asking his…'date'.

Coming to the conclusion that I would rather not try to explain this with dolls in therapy, I hopped on Gabriella, flicked her to life, and left without letting him know.

With the highway near empty, I often broke the speed limit as I rushed to Saint Augustine.

Finding her in tears, she walked with an odd limp. Her black, strapped heels hung from her fingers as she wiped tears from her eyes and whimpered. Pulling alongside her, I parked and helped her up onto my bike.

After fixing her helmet, she tightly wrapped her arms around me. Asking to stop off at her campus for a bit, I lacked the heart to say no to her watery eyes. Once we got there, she wandered over to the concrete benches near Rituals, leaving a trail of spilled tears in her wake.

Sitting, she struggled as she flinched while subconsciously folding her legs. Alarmed by her pain, I sat beside her, "Ella, what's wrong, did someone hurt you?"

"I…" choking on her words, her tears flowed freely off her cheeks as she faked a heart-breaking smile, hoping to convince me that she was all right.

"Who! Who hurt yo…," cutting me off, she looked at me with saddened eyes and sniffled.

"It's not like that. I was with a guy, and we were about to go at it… but he stopped and asked if I mind one of his friends joining us. At first, it was okay, but they got rough…really rough. When it was over, I felt horrible. I wanted it to stop but I couldn't tell them. I hated it, yet I came again and again."

Falling to pieces as she broke down into a sea of tears and uncontrollable crying, she buried her face in my chest. Wrapping her arms around me, in her state of crippling sadness, I was yanked into her mind, seeing the thoughts that were currently in her head.

As darkened flashes flickered, I heard Ella cry out, "Please, don't do this. I'd do anything else, just not this."

Drowned out by a raspy laugh, followed by the distinct sound of a working zipper, I struggled to see who it was through the haze. Coming out of her mind, I knew that what I had just seen was something Ella tried desperately to forget. In her head, it existed as cloudy bits and pieces, but whatever I saw was something that haunted her…something that she tried to bury but could never forget.

Gently prying her off, I placed my hands on her shoulders, looked her in the eyes, and asked, "Did something happen to you when you were younger?"

In an instant, her mood changed. Her sobbing stopped as she wiped away her final tear and instinctively drew her guard. After a moment or two of awkward silence, she faced front, refusing to look at me as she spoke, almost as if she expected to see judgment cast into my eyes.

"It was my uncle…A couple of years ago we all went to a beach house in Tobago. That morning, I didn't know everyone had already left to walk to the beach, everyone except him." Intently listening to her every word, I felt the simmer of my rage grow to a shallow flame, then to a roaring fire.

"After he had his way with me, I was never the same. I just laid there on that bed hoping that it wasn't real…that it didn't just happen. I was so scared of what my family would say that I never told anyone, and I tried to forget it. That's why I decided to pursue psychology. I know now that that incident has a lot to do with my… habits. I hated what happened to me, yet I can't help but be drawn to these men who would completely dominate and use me—men exactly like him! Sometimes I can't even cum unless the sex is forceful. I hate myself for being like this, and you know what the worst part is?… No one cares and they're all too happy to simply label me a slut!"

At that moment I desperately tried to understand what she felt, but I knew I would never truly be able to, so I held her in my arms instead, whispering under my breath, "I care..."

Under the warmth of my jacket, she snuggled as she tried to avoid the gusts of chilly night winds.

"That's why I like you so much."

Confused by her statement, I was left thinking back to our many heated sessions that ended in silence. Before I could ask what she meant, she pulled me from my thoughts as she explained blatantly.

"When we fuck, it feels different. You let me take control and you never make me feel powerless or helpless. Truthfully Darion...the nights you stay over are some of the best ones."

Placing a kiss upon my cheek, she thanked me for picking her up and asked that I stayed the night with her.

After a three-minute ride, we arrived at her apartment building—aside from the chirping crickets, it was lifeless. Parking my bike, we scaled the stairs to her room. With groans of pain, she endured her soreness as she stopped after every stair. Scooping her up, I held her across my arms and made my way to her front door. Attempting to place her into her bed, she playfully refused to release her arms from around my neck.

After a few minutes of light-hearted playing, she stepped into the shower and readied for bed.

Laying down beside me, she rolled into my arms and just stared into my eyes. A bit awkward at first, I quickly felt its allure the longer we laid there. Leaning in, she pressed her soft, tender lips against mine. Slow kisses of the lips soon involved the tongue as she began stripping off my clothes.

Hidden under the sheets, we traced each other's naked bodies with our wandering hands, moaning under the sensations. Remembering her earlier complaints of soreness, I stopped asking if she was still in pain.

Eagerly seeking my lips as I spoke, she said between kisses, "There… are…other things… we could do…that doesn't involve…you going inside of me…"

Reaching for my already hard cock, I stopped her, smiled, and said, "You had a rough night, let me take care of you."

Not trying to be an insensitive ass, my use of the word rough momentarily flooded me with cringy regret, but she paid it no mind.

Kissing her, I lightly nibbled her bottom lip before making my way to her neck. Placing kiss after kiss against her flesh, I worked my way down slowly, until her perfectly perky tits came into view. Wrapping my lips around her right nipple, I swirled it against my tongue as I rolled the other between my fingertips. With my face gleefully on her breasts, it was easy to tell that her tension was building. Her heavy breathing became some of the sweetest moans ever uttered as her rising pleasure intoxicated me…encouraged me.

Switching between her nipples as I gladly moved from breast to breast, I slid my fingers along her toned stomach, trailing her landing strip before sliding between the lips of her wet slit. Careful not to penetrate her by accident, I made sure she was dripping wet before kissing along her stomach and over her mound. Brushing the tip of my tongue against her pussy, her body spasmed from the unexpected sensation.

Gradually working my lips around her clit, I massaged it with the gentle motions of my tongue as her nectar trailed happily along my chin. With her fingers finding their way into my hair, her tightening grip hailed the coming of her orgasm as her hips experienced random spasms of uncontrollable pleasure. I saw her stomach tense up as she curled forward. Locking gazes at the perfect time, I saw the raw, uninhibited waves of ecstasy crash in her eyes as she soaked her mattress. Crawling from beneath the covers, I slid next to her wiping her orgasm from my lips.

Seizing the opportunity, Ella rolled into my arms and lulled off to sleep.

Brushing her hair from her face as she dreamt, I recalled my first impression of her, after diving into her most vulgar thoughts. Given what she had told me earlier, I felt ample self-loathing knowing that I had judged her so harshly and quickly. All this time I thought that I was just another boy toy on her long list—instead, I was the only one that helped how she felt about herself. In the sea of my misguided actions and intentions, I managed to pay her a kindness. That night, unlike those prior, I gladly held her as she slept, feeling a desperate need inside of me to take all her pain away.

As the minutes marched on, I too fell into slumber's grasp.

Chapter Seven

A screaming voice thick with rage and frustration rattled through Ella's apartment as the beams of the morning sun tore through the panes of her window.

"Darion, get out here!"

Pulled from sleep, we both woke up to the wails of a furious Zatanni fiddling with his keys to get in. The look on his face as he burst through the door immediately flooded the room with the stench of my betrayal. Rushing to my feet, I prepared for the worst as Ella attempted to quell the situation.

"Get the hell out of my sister's apartment!" he barked as I tried to explain myself.

With a single swing, I was given a busted lip and tossed to the ground. Amidst Ella's frantic cries for Zatanni to stop, I struggled back up to my feet and prepared to retaliate. Forcing myself to stop my fist, I lowered my hand.

"I deserved that, and I'm sorry."

I battled to look him in the eye.

Shoving Ella aside, he grabbed me by the neck and warned me to stay the hell away from his sister. With a hard push, I was shoved out of the apartment as Zatanni continued his scolding behind closed doors.

While being gawked at by the prying eyes of nosey neighbors, I hopped on my bike and rode home, replaying everything in my head and fighting the shooting pain in my jaw. That night, as I tossed and turned amongst my ruffled blanket, I felt the wretched guilt of my betrayal keeping me awake. The tick of the clock on my wall became deafening while the look on Zatanni's face was burned into my mind.

Vibrating in one of the many folds of my covers, I searched for my phone, wondering who was calling at three in the morning. Surprised, I felt a sinking feeling in my gut, seeing Zatanni's name appear on the caller ID. Expecting a tongue lashing, I answered to the sorrowful voice of Ella.

"Darion, I'm sorry but I can't see you anymore. Zatanni made me give up my apartment, he took my phone and said that he'd drop and pick me up from my classes from now on. Sorry for the trouble I caused but thank you for all that you did."

I saw her only a hand full of times after that day.

Nearing the third week of silence, the unanswered calls and texts made me worrisome. I would be lying if I said my urgency to hear from her didn't stem from a newfound desire to protect her. Between what she told me and what I saw in her mind that night, the thought of someone having to bear that torment alone or at all, showered me with indescribable sorrow. I was one of the only persons she had ever told. I felt so helpless not being able to change that horrid thing that happened to her, while at the same time wanting to ensure nothing like that ever happened to her again. Was I wrong for seeing her as this fragile thing? Was I misguided for wanting to protect her? It was questions like these that drove me to go check on her.

One evening, I rode into her campus. Timing her classes and the evening traffic, I managed to arrive half an hour before her class was let out. In an attempt to kill some time, I bought a White Chocolate Chiller from Rituals. The wait in line was more than enough to make me late. Scampering back to my bike, I made it just in time to see Zatanni pulling up.

I felt fear whip my chest as I froze momentarily from its sharp sting. Internalizing my panic, I nonchalantly approached Gabriella and tossed my leg over her. From the corner of my eye, I saw Zatanni facing me, and I felt his glare through the visor of his helmet.

Like clockwork, his arrival signaled the end of Ella's classes.

With a small smile, her face momentarily lit up at the sight of me. Like a snowflake on warm skin, the beauty of her joy was brief and was instantly replaced by a blank expression and unhappy eyes. Mounting her brother's motorcycle, she managed to wave goodbye to me as they rode off.

After that day, it would be months before I saw her again. During that time, I attempted to nurse my heart back from yet another heartbreak. It sucked...getting to see the depths of someone's life and experience them laying their secrets bare before you, only to have them yanked away. Like a snapping rubber band, we both felt its sting and suffered in the resounding ripples of pain.

I missed her, even more so than I did Miss Alysandra—something that, up until that moment, I thought was impossible.

Comparing how I felt about Miss Aly to Ella, I realized that what I felt for my teacher was not love at all. Instead, it was the hooks of an adult woman tugging on the mind of a naive young man.

It was the first time I felt a bond like this with someone on an emotional level. A heat, different from that which came from the pleasures of the flesh, radiated through my chest every time I thought of Ella.

At first, I had no idea what exactly I was feeling, but the more I thought about it and her, the more I realized that I was falling in love. I felt as though I was suffering from some warped form of the Florence Nightingale Effect. Not only did I want to help her, but I fell in love with the idea of keeping her safe.

Was I misguided in my thinking? She managed to survive the best way she knew how up until now.

I tried to justify the insignificance of myself in her life, hoping that it would do something to ease the heartache of not being able to see her.

After a month of complete silence on their paths, I got a call from a number I did not recognize. It was around five on a Wednesday evening when my phone rang. Busy working on my bike, I almost didn't answer in time. Bringing the phone to my ear, I felt my heart plunge to hear Ella incoherently crying. Finding out where she was, I jumped on Gabriella as she roared to life. Speeding off, I chased my worry and rage along the highway until I got to her campus.

There was a bar within walking distance from the university that shared a carpark with the campus. Pulling in, I cruised along the rows of vehicles until I saw Ella crying. With her face on her knees, she was tucked away at the far corner of the car park. Hustling to get off my bike, I practically sprinted over to her. "Ella...Ella what's wrong?" When she lifted her head, I felt all shreds of rational thought get scorched from my skull. With a swollen face, she cried as she told me that the guy who had roughed her up that night wanted to have more fun with her and a few of his friends. After she repeatedly

Dimitri Valentene

said no to him, he grabbed her wrist and she tossed her drink in his face. That was when he slapped her and called her a slut.

Fishing what I needed out of the tool bag on my bike, I left Ella in the carpark, walked into the bar, and shouted, "Hey! Anyone here knows a girl named Ella?"

With my question being met with little interest, one guy did utter a loud enough comment to draw my attention.

"Who did the slut screw now!"

He laughed with his two friends.

That was all the proof I needed.

Walking up to him and his buddies, I dropped the wrench hidden behind my right arm into view. Before they could explain, I started swinging and did not stop until they were all unconscious on the floor. I had no idea what came over me—it was as if I was not in control of myself at all. All I wanted to do was make them pay.

It did not take long for the police to arrive and arrest me then and there.

While they guided me out in handcuffs, I saw Zatanni looking over Ella's face in the car park. From where I was, I could tell he was asking her who hurt her. Pointing in my direction, she guided him to the three guys being brought out on stretchers by the paramedics.

A few hours after I was booked at the police station, I received a visit from Zatanni. Talking to me through the bars of my holding cell, I could see it in his eyes what he had to tell me was difficult to say.

"Thank you...for looking out for Ella. I'm glad she had you to call. I sure as hell know she would've never told me what happened."

"Nah...Don't worry about it buddy...Someone had to teach those dicks a lesson."

I tried to be cool, knowing it would ease the tension that he was feeling.

"Look, you're a good guy Darion, but as my friend, you should have just told me. I can't trust you, and if I don't trust you as a friend, I can't trust you with my little sister."

With bated breath, I attempted to refute his point, but no words would slip past my lips—my mind was blank.

He was right.

The reason for my silence in this crucial moment was because he was right. I knew then and there if I had ever considered him a friend, the least I could do was respect his wishes and stay away from Ella...so I did.

Threatening to take the three guys to court for the assault on his sister, she decided to leave them be if they dropped their charges against me. After that, I did my best to refrain from seeing her. I was successful for nearly six months, right up until I got accepted into the University of Trinidad and Tobago, Point Lisas campus.

The day I received my acceptance letter and student package, my dad decided to celebrate. Successful with my application to their diploma program, I was set to study mechanical engineering in the coming school year. Bringing along his date and her daughter, my dad insisted we visit a nightclub in South Trinidad called Space. Feeling a bit dated that my dad knew what or where Space nightclub was and I didn't, made it hard to deny that he lived a more avid life than I did.

Tailing him and his date as we drove along the highway, I was pleasantly surprised when we arrived. The club seemed nice and lively as we ventured to the back of the line. It did not take long for the sports bike in the carpark to catch my eye. A black and gold Ninja 250 sitting like the stunning beauty she was under one of few lights illuminating the car park. Overall, the club had a nice vibe—strobing lights, dancing, and alcohol made for a great night.

A night that got even better the moment I saw her dancing in the crowd. Consumed by a bubbling excitement, I was genuinely happy to see Ella's beautiful face for the first time in months.

Chapter Eight

I t was not long before she noticed, walked over and hooked her arm around mine. Josie, the daughter of my dad's date, was less than pleased after sticking to me like glue most of the night.

Getting to spend time with Ella was like a glass of cool water after a gruelling trek through the scorching desert, and being away from Josie was just the ice cube to top it all off.

When we finally sifted through the dancing crowd and got to the bar, Ella yelled our order over the blaring music. As she shared a laugh with the bartender, I looked at the smile on her happy face and felt the ease of contentment within that moment. I was happy to simply be near her and I knew she felt the same. After introducing me to the two friends she came with, we chugged our drinks and chipped over to the dancefloor.

Dressed in a simple fitted vest, her legs were wrapped in leather pants and red strapped heels adorned her feet. Though she was not dressed the fanciest, her sensual moves on the dance floor as she often trailed her figure with her fingers, gathered her most of the attention.

I'm sure she caused more than a few guys with wandering eyes to be smacked by their jealous girlfriends.

As we danced, time did not fade…instead, it just failed to matter.

Each second staring at her face as we moved was more blissful than the last. No one else mattered—it was just me, her, and the music. With song after song encouraging sweet wines and less than wholesome dancing, a rather slow song came across the speakers "You and Me" by Lifehouse. Shying away, I inched to leave the dance floor. Not knowing much about slow dancing, I shuddered at the thought of making a fool of myself.

Stopping me in my tracks, Ella worked me into her arms as she rested her head against my chest and guided me. Gently swaying from side to side, I heard her say, "That's one of the things I love most about you, you never mind me taking control."

Through My Eyes – The First Five

With a rush of joy that I did my best to internalize, I held her tighter, fighting the urge to ask and probably ruin the moment, "You love me?" Figuring it was better left unsaid, I simply enjoyed our dance. As the song played its last few seconds, she looked up from my chest, sighed happily with a smile, and kissed me across my lips.

A rush flooded through my very being.

Ensnared in her arms and locked against her lips, the idea that I was in a club eagerly fell from my thoughts. Tracing her back with my hands, I slid them to her leather-wrapped cheeks, squeezing her ass as I pulled her hips into mine. Little did I know I had just started a roaring fire within Ella...a fire that she intended to quell with my body.

There was a section inside of Space Nightclub that had long leather couches. With her legs over me, and her practically sitting in my lap, we kissed hard and heavy as she pushed me deeper into the black leather. With every shift, the upholstery complacently squeaked. It often pulled me from the heat of the moment and made me wonder about the silent sins that this corner of the club had witnessed.

Growing frustrated by the winey leather, Ella got up and pulled me in the direction of the washrooms. Turning the corner, we were met by a brooding bouncer whose face implied he knew exactly what we were up to. His muscles implied that we should turn around, so we did.

Having one last stroke of genius, I was once again guided by her grip as we waded through the sea of people, making our way to her friends. Whispering something into one of their ears, both peered at me and shared a giggle.

Handing Ella the car keys, her near drunk friend gave me a look that suggested 'Bow chicca wow wow' was playing in her head. Keen on what we were about to do in her car, she seemed too enticed by her drink to pay mind to anything else.

Still following her lead, we made our way to the carpark. As we approached a grey Subaru wagon, she broke the silence that loomed over our eagerness. "You like my bike?" she asked, pointing to the black and gold ninja parked under the light pole. Surprised that it was hers, I was even more shocked that Zatanni had bought it for her.

"It's almost as sexy as its rider," I said as the drinks we had earlier fostered my false confidence.

"I know you're probably thinking that I could have easily come to see you... at first, that was all I wanted to do, but Zatanni installed a GPS. The deal was, I had to leave it on if I wanted the bike. Some freedom was better than none at the time."

Before the guilt could set in over what she told me, she unlocked the car, opened the door, and hauled me in. As I pulled the door shut behind us, all manner of sound fell dead and both of us were plunged into a world of silence.

Through the dim glow of the club lights that shimmered their way into the car, the once quiet stillness was replaced by overzealous kissing and the removal of anything that hindered the writhing of our naked bodies. Drawing her vest over her shoulders, she stripped me of my shirt as she lay back into the seat, pulling me over her. Tossing her bra to the front seat, she graced me with the sight of her perky breasts and light brown nipples. Seeing her busty chest after so long, prompted me to say the single stupidest thing I had ever said. After licking both her nipples, I looked up at her as the words sprang to life, "I really did miss my breast friends."

Bursting into laughter, it took a couple moments before she settled down. Cuddling for a bit, she ran her fingers along my stomach before sighing, "I missed this."

Pulling my face, she resumed our kissing as I made it a priority for my lips to touch every inch of her skin. Leisurely, I worked down her body, dragging my lips as her aroma uncaged the lusting beast within me. Pouncing, my playful kisses sharpened to bites, each causing her moans to grow louder.

Unbuttoning her pants, I slid them down only to be faulted by her strapped, red heels. Clumsily removing her shoes and relieving her of her leather pants, I scaled her smooth, toned legs with my eyes. Aroused by my fiery stares as I perused her bare skin, she opened her legs to give me a better view of her laced panties being eaten by her luscious lips.

Sitting upright, Ella slid back and hooked her ankles on the shoulders of the two front seats. Pulling me in with her finger and seductive eyes, she brought me to my knees in the legroom of the back seat. Though it was a tight fit and a bit uncomfortable, I could not have cared less. Sitting inches away from her snatch, it was not long before her scent hooked my nose and drew my mouth in for a taste.

I leaned in close enough that she felt the rush of every breath I took as it brushed past her eagerly glistening slit. From her slow squirms and her drooling pussy, I could tell that her want made her impatient. Quickly deciding that she had waited long enough, she knotted her fingers through my hair and roped me in. A smack echoed as soon as her taste flowed past my lips. Like a recovering addict that scored a fix, that first taste of her pushed a muffled, "Mmmmmhh," past my lips.

Gripping the tender flesh of her thighs, my hands made their way to her ass as I grabbed handfuls of her supple cheeks. Prodding her hole with my tongue, I slid it in and out as her wetness coated the lower half of my face. Pushing her legs up from the shoulders of the front seats, I gripped behind her knees and held them further apart, allowing me to bury my face deeper into her cunt. Moaning freely, she sang me the songs of her sensual pleasure, caring little about who else may overhear.

Using her grip on my hair, she pulled me away from her intoxicating juices to stick her tongue in my mouth and bite at my bottom lip. Fiddling with my buckle, she eventually managed to undo my belt and slide my pants off. Stopping for a moment I felt the stinging slap of disappointment.

"Ella, I don't have a condom."

Pulling me to sit beside her, she got on all fours on the seat. Taking my throbbing cock in her hand, she lowered her head as she teased, "Don't worry about that, I'm back on the pill. Besides, I want to feel every inch of you tonight."

Hearing her say that she was back on the pill struck me as odd, but before I could raise a question, the waves of pleasure that rippled through my body when her lips wrapped around the head of my dick washed all rational thoughts from my mind. With her bobbing head and warm tongue driving an incredible sensation between my legs, I moaned in bliss.

"Fuck…your lips are to die for!"

With my pink head still kissed against her lips and teeth, she smiled and said that she told me so. After a chuckle, she worked my rod with intent. Slurping as she drooled along my shaft, she stroked and sucked, egging my building orgasm.

Tossing her leg over me, she lowered herself onto my stiff rod, stuffing inch after inch of me into her warm insides. Once I was all the way in, she wrapped her arms around my neck and leaned back. Grinding her hips, I felt my cock being gripped by the walls of her stretching hole.

As our rising pleasure soared to astounding heights, our soulful moans and the heat of our writhing bodies condensed the cold night air on the car windows. Her grinding hips bounced as the vulgar sounds of slapping flesh coupled with our moans. Feeling the sharp stabs of Ella's nails as she clawed my back, the moans she uttered in my ear made the pain worth it.

Lifting her up, I placed her on her back. Looming over her, we locked eyes as I slid my cock back into her open hole. With her legs and arms, she wrapped herself around me as my hips thrusted. Each stroke into her dribbling cunt was met with a resounding slush that sounded wetter the harder we fucked. I felt the sting as my sweat seeped into the nail marks along my back. Fighting through the pain, I pounded her pussy until I felt her walls grip tightly on my shaft. Knowing that she was about to climax, I continued my assault on her pussy as the pleasurable pulses of her orgasm prompted me to spray every drop of cum I had into her.

When we were finally finished, we did not bother heading back into the club. Instead, we stayed in the car wrapped in each other's arms until her friends were ready to leave, dreading the moment we had to part ways again. Sharing one last kiss, we both mounted our bikes and rode off. It was hard saying goodbye that night, but the days after got easier. In some way, I had gotten closure from our wild time. Though my wounds soon started healing, the feelings never faded, and Ella forged a special place in my heart.

With the two weeks I had off before I was expected to start classes at the university, my dad wanted to do something together as father and son. Deciding we should get tattoos—an idea that came from his 'companion'—it was something I wanted to do at least once before I kicked it. As soon as I laid eyes on the drawing, I knew I had to get it.

I love the idea of something pure looking after me all the time, especially while I was on my bike. I took a tattoo of a faceless angel on my right arm while dad got a skull and crossbones inked on his chest. Aside from that, the rest of my gap year was quiet. I missed Ella a lot, but with the passing days, her absence hurt less and less. By the time the school year commenced, my tattoo was fully healed, and I had entered yet another chapter of my life and sexual journey within the walls of the University of Trinidad and Tobago.

Chapter Nine
Tertiary Level Sex Ed

When I started college, I was more than lost—the sheer size of the campus did little for my disorientation. On my first day, I casually walked past the gates only to be apprehended by a security guard. Making me sign my name and student ID number, she paid me a smile and sent me on my way.

Making it past the student accounting office, I walked into the auditorium by mistake. The icy rush of the air conditioning blasted me as all eyes were drawn to the opening door in my grip. Silently I pulled back and left feeling a bit out of place.

The sound of dragging chairs to my right, brought me to a door that had the word 'café' sprawled across its glass. Unlike the auditorium, the café was warm. It was something I had to quickly get used to since the university never seemed to have money to get it fixed. Placing my helmet on one of the many tables set in rows amongst a sea of chairs, I unzipped my jacket as my gear drew a few questions from fresh year ones seeking to make friends on their first day. After engaging in polite conversation for a few minutes, I saw the masses funnelling through the café doors. Accustomed to the signal of the school bell, I was a bit lost as to what the hell was going on at first.

Realizing that classes had started, I fiddled with my timetable as I navigated the 'old building' trying to find my classroom. The structure of the campus was simple...after I explored enough. There were two buildings that held classes—one was constructed a couple of years after the other and by default was dubbed by students and faculty as 'the new building'. In between both were the auditorium and café that lead outside to rows of concrete tables with adjoining benches. Back when I started, this area was called 'the smoke shed'—it was a place students would go and smoke a cigarette between and after classes before the university got stricter with its rules.

Set near the industrial estate in Point Lisas, bars, restaurants and even small malls were no more than a five-minute ride away. Not as sprawling at the grounds of UWI, UTT was still a nice place to be.

During my first class, I could tell that the lecturer had little experience with female students. His lewd jokes and blatant comments felt out of place to the three girls that were in our class. Knowing that we were all unfamiliar with each other, Mr. Batoo along with most of our lecturers that week placed us into groups to see how well we worked with our peers.

Unlike most of the guys in my class, I was not too thrilled to have one of the three girls in my group. Don't get me wrong, the girls at my campus were at the top of their classes, but there were some that sailed through on their charms, good looks, and willingness to send nudes to have their name put on the paper. This fact made me skeptical about my female groupmate.

Calling from his list of names, he rattled them off in threes as each of us raised our hands so others would know who we were. Luckily, I was able to avoid that awkward roam through the classroom to find my group members because we were already sitting right next to each other.

Giving him a glance and a head-bob of approval, I felt someone touch my shoulder. Through the chatter and shuffling chairs, a meek voice just barely made it to my ears.

"Are you Darion? Hi, I'm Ellisia...but my friends call me Elli."

Mistakenly hearing Ella, I felt the rapid rise of my happiness and the even quicker descent into disappointment as I spun around. Swaddled in a pink, fluffy jacket, streams of her thick frizzy hair flowed along both sides of her face from under her hood. Her oddly pale skin highlighted the many freckles of her cheeks while her thick, rounded glasses drew to the subtle beauty of the green flecks in her hazel eyes. Admittingly hearing Ella instead of Elli had put me in a bad mood—I knew days like this were unavoidable and I really should have thought about my response…but before I could stop myself, I spoke out of frustration.

"Don't worry, I'd never call you Elli."

My harsh tongue did all but cast tears into her eyes as she dragged a chair over to sit with us.

I won't lie, I felt horrible for what I said, but the crashing waves of contemplation, over the situation with Ella and me kept me near-silent for the rest of the class. When the lecturer finally dismissed us, I grabbed my bag and left in a hurry. Hopping on my bike, I rode out the school gates.

With the chaotic bombardment of the thoughts in my mind, I felt myself slipping deeper into sadness. Aimlessly riding, I got lost netted in the maze-like backroads of California. I rode until I met a bar hidden away in a dead-end street—painted above its entrance was the name Silverado. Well hidden, it was the local watering hole for older students who had been exploring the area well over a year. As I pulled up, Gabriella did what she does best. Gathering me the attention of the two small groups sitting on the rounded concrete tables under Carib umbrellas, their tracking eyes were as good as pointed fingers.

Making my way inside, it looked and smelled like all bars did, except this one was filled with solely UTT students. It was easy to tell because most of them had the bright red strings of their student IDs still hanging around their necks. Paying their eyes little mind, it was not until I got to the bar that I realized my helmet was still on. All eyes were on me as I pulled up and walked in, probably because they thought I was going to rob the place. Finally removing it from my head, I set it down at the counter and ordered a Stag from the barkeep. As I drank, its soothing chill felt satisfying…and with three in a row, its alcohol numbed my mind and hushed my thoughts.

"Nice bike."

A deep voice rung from behind me.

"She's yours?" a rather tall and bulky guy asked.

"Yeah, I restored her close to a year ago, her name's Gabriella."

Laughing at the fact that she had his ex-girlfriend's name, he pulled the chair beside me and sat down, telling me that his name was Rudras. Before I could say two words to him, a girl about half his size, with a nip in her hands plopped next to him. She had fair skin and wavy hair that ended an inch or two before her shoulders. Her name was Manda but everyone called her Mandy for some reason. Best friends—they were an odd pairing. Loving to drink, Mandy never refused a trip to the bar, but Rudras never drank. Instead, he often took care of Mandy during her drunken charades. Both enrolled in the University's Degree Program, they were much older than I was, but they were a pair of the kindest and most warm-hearted individuals I had ever met.

After downing a beer as Mandy mixed drinks from her nip of White Oak, we ventured back to campus for afternoon classes. Reaching a bit late, I was not the last one to walk in. The beers I had drank still lingered on my breath and fondly riddled my senses.

Minutes after I took my seat at the only empty desk, Ellisia traipsed through the door. With little choice, the looks on our faces made our displeasure obvious as she dropped her bag onto the other half of my desk. That evening our entire class had the pleasure of sitting through a seminar that covered the transition to university life. It was all standard boring stuff so the lack of engagement through the entire thing weighed heavy on my eyelids. I fought my drooping head, counting the minutes as the clock ticked.

My attention was everywhere else, up until the moment the presenter spoke about sexual assault and harassment. Her words woke the flashes that I saw the night Ella told me what had happened with her uncle. With the influence of alcohol flowing through my veins and the daze of my boredom-induced drowsiness, I felt as if I was there. Vividly playing in my head, all elements of the classroom vanished. I was plunged into darkness as I heard Ella cry out. I felt her fear and pain—I felt the torment of her memories. Locked in my vision, I saw nothing but deep darkness. Unknowingly, I tightened my grip on the edge of the desk, my trembling hands shaking it, pulling Ellisia's attention. Overwhelmed by the rush of emotions that flooded me, tears flowed from my eyes. Attempting to pull me from my trance, Ellisia grabbed my hand. At that moment, I felt the mountain of pain and sorrow that was crushing me, cut in half. As Ella's voice faded, I came too at the end of the seminar to see the fear and bewilderment on Ellisia's face as she cupped her right hand. Her shocked and terrified look was followed by a single question— "Who is Ella?"

Unsure if she had seen what I saw, I grabbed my helmet, shoved my way through the door, and darted down the hallway. Tailing me, she called out many times, but I did my best to ignore the sounds of her voice. When we finally got to the carpark, she stood in front of my bike and refused to move unless I gave her answers. Though her persistence was admirable, I found it beyond infuriating at the time.

Giving her a fierce look that prompted her to step back, I ground my teeth and yelled, "You know nothing about me, so just leave me the fuck alone…Okay? And never say her name again!"

With tears in her eyes, I was beyond remorseful that I had made her cry, but glad when she moved out of my way.

After slowly moving through the week, Friday came—I had the joy of knowing that Ellisia was in every single one of my classes. Making for more than a few awkward moments, aside from group work, we did our best to avoid each other.

Through My Eyes – The First Five

At the end of my first week being a university student, I decided to celebrate with a stop at Silverado. Pulling up, I was greeted by Rudras drinking a Pepsi and Mandy halfway through her first bottle. Welcoming me with open arms, they introduced me to their friends who quickly mixed me a drink. Trying my best to keep up, I desperately wanted to avoid being viewed as the baby of the bunch. As the hours passed, I realized more and more how stupid I was for embarking on that venture.

In a near drunken state, I was in no condition to ride. One by one, Rudras, Mandy, and their friends went home, and I was left contemplating a life-threatening decision. Thinking about nothing other than getting home, I carelessly decide to approach my bike. Before I could start Gabriella, I was stopped. Taking my keys in her hand, Ellisia shook her head as she looked at me. Nearly stumbling over, she managed to hold my weight up with her petite frame. Mounting the motorcycle, she secured me to her back and wrapped my arms around her waist. Urging my bike to life, she skilfully maneuvered the back streets as I clung to her like a baby chimpanzee.

I don't know exactly why I did it…perhaps I was just being perverted, but I jumped at the opportunity and dove into her most private and vulgar thoughts.

Thrown into a dimly lit bedroom, Ellisia was wrapped up under her covers while porn played on the laptop next to her. With her frizzy hair spread wildly across her pillow, her head tossed and turned while her hands worked tirelessly between her legs. Moaning softly, masked by her covers, she pleasured herself as she fingered her pussy and fondled her petite breasts. Paying little attention to her laptop, her tightly shut eyes suggested that she was deep in her fantasy.

With climbing moans that proposed she was close, she stopped abruptly to change positions. Bending over, she draped her blanket across her back before fishing in her nightstand. Pulling out an average-sized, purple dildo, she spun its base causing it to hum to life. Guiding her hands underneath the sheets, I saw her body spasm at the sensation of her toy's first touch. Moaning into her pillow, she gradually got louder, doing her best to muffle her sweltering sounds. Her bed gently rocked, and the slushing noises of her working hole chimed in. Her spasms got closer together as a shallow wail of ecstasy parted her lips. Furiously she toyed her slit until her sweet release, cumming as her body spasmed on the vibrator buried within her pussy.

After diving into her mind, I did not remember much of what happened after. The next morning when I woke up in Ellisia's bed to the sounds of someone knocking against her front door.

Chapter Ten

D azed by the mist of my hangover, it took me a minute or two to realize where I was. When she opened her front door, a guy stepped in, spread his arms, and hollered in a rather deep voice, "Fear not my sweet, for Vik is here."

The best way that I could describe him is pretty— gorgeous even…for a guy that is. He was just shy of six feet tall, fair skin that easily got red in the sun while his head of short, tightly wound, sugar-colored curls complimented his dark brown eyes. In a low-hanging black V-neck, he proudly displayed the tattoo on his chest. Halted by the sight of me standing in the bedroom doorway, he lifted an eyebrow before petting Ellisia's head.

89

"My my my… Hey babe? Looks like Elli has company—rather fine company at that."

Rendered mute by his comment, his girlfriend, Bell, stepped in to see what the fuss was about. In a pair of baggy track pants that slung off her hips and a fitted white vest, her hair was tied in a bun with a pair of darkened sunglasses across her eyes that partially hid a scar above her eyebrow. Lowering them, she peered over the frame and proceeded with the same reaction as Vik.

"My my…holding out on us Elli?"

"Guys it's not like that!"

Her freckles faded into her reddening cheeks.

Nursing the headache that was rattling my skull and not knowing what to make of the entire situation, I grabbed my helmet and jacket and headed towards the door.

Passing Ellisia as I left, all I could say was, "See you in school on Monday."

Hopping on Gabriella, I turned her key. I sat in silence as I cleared my head for the ride home.

Sadly, my entire weekend was unwillingly dedicated to wallowing in sadness as I fought the urge to visit Ella. Having wronged Zatanni once, I did not think I could bear the guilt of a second betrayal. With a yearning that was unsatisfiable, I replayed the steamy night she and I shared at the back of her friend's car. Closing my eyes, I saw her ankles hooked on the two front seats. Stroking my cock, I masturbated countless times trying to appease my desire.

Playing her voice as she moaned, remembering how she smelled, tasted, and felt, provided for one intense orgasm after the next.

Eventually Monday rolled around, despite my wishes for an eternal weekend. Not knowing what to say to Ellisia, I dreaded going to my classes, seeing that she was in every one of them. After Friday night and how I reacted Saturday morning, I knew that I did not want to face her, but I didn't want to ditch classes either. Stuck in a conundrum, I decided to reach an hour late hoping to avoid any pre-class conversation before the teacher got there.

Given my luck with the universe, when I arrived at ten for my nine-a.m. class, the only available seat was next to Ellisia. At that moment, I wished I was better at math—that way I could have calculated the odds of having to sit next to her, even though I knew this was just karma flipping me off.

Taking my seat, I rummaged through my backpack for my notebook and pen. The first few minutes were spent trying to understand what was on the whiteboard. My best guess was that it was something they found on the alien ships that crashed in Roswel.

Beyond lost, I regretted missing the first hour of class. Running my fingers through my hair, my visible frustration prompted Ellisia to slide her notes across the table. Looking at her book, then at her as she paid full mind to our lecturer, I wondered, "Why does she keep being nice to me? Even after all I've said and the asinine way I behaved, she would still help me."

Seeing that I was staring at her from the corner of her eyes, she turned. Paying her an honest smile, I saw her face light up. In her short flare of joy, I felt like I was really seeing her for the first time as she smiled a wide, bright smile. Though she looked simple and average, Ellisia was quite pretty. Not flashy in any way though— her beauty resounded in her simplicity.

After class, she waited for me near the door, ambushing me as soon as I left the classroom. Given that she took care of me on Friday night, and saved me from possibly crashing my bike, I figured I owed her an explanation. In silence, we made our way between the buildings and strolled over to the 'smoke shed'.

"Thanks... for taking my keys Friday." I said as we sat.

"You shouldn't be drinking and riding!" she reprimanded as the sharpness of her serious tone cut into me.

Shocked, I stared at her wondering what I could have possibly said to get her upset, but before I could apologize, she did.

"Sorry, I didn't mean to yell. My brother was a rider, he loved motorcycles, a bit too much for his own good."

Cutting her off, I asked, "Is that how you learned to ride? With your brother?"

"Yes, he taught me when he got his first bike. There was no better feeling than riding with him, cruising along the roads as the wind rushes past you. Those were some of the best times I had ever had. When my brother died last year, it all stopped, and mom didn't want to see or hear anything about me being near a motorcycle again."

Lost for words, I uttered the go-to line in that situation.

"I'm sorry for your loss."

With nothing else that I could say, I hated that all I had to offer was that hallow sentence. Seeing the tears welled in her eyes and knowing that my words offered little comfort, I reached over and held her hand. Soft and cold to the touch, I immediately understood why she always wore that fluffy pink hoodie.

"Two antennas got married…," befuddled by my random statement, her facial expression screamed, "What the hell are you talking about?!"

"Two antennas got married…the wedding was crap, but the reception was great!"

Erupting into laughter, my poor attempt at humor prolonged our conversation. Completely forgetting about our afternoon class, Ellisia and I sat and spoke for hours as her once dismal mood slowly shifted.

93

"What's the deal with Vik?"

My question prompted her to go off on a tangent about her friends. "Vik is short for Viktor—Bell's boyfriend and part two of my two-part best friend. He's been in my life for as long as I could remember." Making a comment that I found him a bit flamboyant, Ellisia informed me that he was bisexual and so was Bell. Remembering how she looked that day, I did think that her style was a bit masculine. It explained why she dressed and spoke the way she did. Not that I was judging—she seemed great.

All three of them grew up together and after attending the same primary and secondary schools, they parted ways when Ellisia enrolled in UTT and they got accepted to attend UWI. Refusing to lose contact, they all ensured that they were always avid parts of each other's lives.

Enthralled by our conversation that seemed to transcend time, the sky had already begun to darken and the winds grew colder as they howled through the canefield near campus. With the part-time students scurrying off to their classes, the thought of heading home crossed my mind. When I was about to tell her I was ready to leave, she asked the question I dreaded.

"Darion...Who's Ella?"

Expecting her to eventually bring it up didn't help the sharp stab I felt in my chest when her words fell upon my ears.

"Ella was a friend of mine. I met her about a year ago…before I started university."

This was the first time I had spoken to anyone about Ella. Hearing her name slip past my lips riddled my voice with cracks as the honesty about my feeling lingered on my words while I spoke.

"Did someone hurt her?"

I knew then and there she saw exactly what I had seen that evening. What happened to Ella was not my business to tell, but to appease Ellisia's question, I told her that she was hurt by someone she thought she could have trusted. Vague enough to keep her wondering, she asked the other question I feared answering.

"What happened that day when I touched your hand? It freaked me out! I saw flashes, I heard horrible things and I felt this mountain of pain and suffering that was not mine."

Against my better judgment and the advice of every superhero origin movie ever, I told her almost everything. I started at the accident, explaining to her how I first got my powers and about the things I could do. Once I started talking, I just continued for hours. Uncontrollably, I bore my life's story to Ellisia. Though I wanted to stop myself many times, her attentive silence made it impossible.

By the time I was finished, she knew about my abilities, bits of what ensued with Miss Alysandra, and everything that happened with me and Ella. After my rambling and her promising not to tell a soul, she said nothing about Ella, but her thoughts towards Miss Alysandra were the same as Zatanni's—she too believed that I was taken advantage of.

When we finally got up to leave, she stopped me and asked one last question.

"Darion... have you ever looked into my mind?"

Bringing images of her bent over under her blanket, and masturbating with her purple dildo to mind, I swallowed hard. Licking my lips, as all men did before they lied, I smiled and told her no. While walking off, she invited me to come out with her friends Bell and Viktor on Friday to check out a club they had heard about.

Chapter Eleven

For the rest of that week, I was more than happy to sit next to Ellisia for all my classes. Feeling a serene sense of ease and peace when around her, the pains that once plucked at my heartstrings slowly lost their will to do so—hurtful memories were replaced with happy ones.

Heartaches, when you are young, are like fireworks—they burn bright and leave an impression, but eventually they all fade, and new fireworks go off.

When we were not locked in lectures, we ate lunch together—I even introduced her to Rudras and Mandy. Not much of a drinker, she kept Rudras company while Mandy and I tried to out-drink each other.

Dimitri Valentene

When Friday came, I left home around six in the evening. Letting Gabriella loose on the highway, I swerved in and out of cars as I made my way to The Rise. An average-sized bar and restaurant near Price Plaza, nights there would always end in drunken dancing and pleasantly embarrassing memories. The crowd that frequented there was friendly and often approachable enough to engage in conversation with.

Though this was my first time there, it was definitely not my last and became somewhat of a habit on a Friday evening.

When I arrived, Ellisia, Vik, and Bell already had a table near the bar, with an empty chair waiting for me. Waving me over, I saw Bell whispering something to Ellisia that flushed her freckled face as I approached.

Wrapped in a fitted black dress, its thin straps cradled her shoulders. Clinging to her body and the tiny yet noticeable punch of her tummy, it highlighted the figure she kept blanketed under her fluffy hoodie. Framing her waist, her dress flared at her surprisingly wide hips and luscious ass. Her once frizzy hair was now a full set of tamed curls that draped over her shoulders, drawing eyes to her near flat chest. Without her glasses, her contacts made the flecks of green against the hazel of her eyes look even more mesmerizing.

Pulling my chair, I sat in between her and Viktor. Admittingly, after recalling Ellisia telling me he was bisexual, my shield of masculinity was up at full strength.

Throughout the night, though it was never warranted, I kept Viktor at the corner of my eye.

After a few drinks, the mist of awkward silence lifted as we regaled one another with experiences from our lives. When we were about three beers in, Vik fancied a smoke and sought me as his company to stroll outside. Hesitant, I was short on excuses, so I had no choice but to tag along. Clicking his plastic lighter, he struggled to light his cigarette against the unwavering wind. Moving in closer, I positioned myself to ease the gusts long enough for him to get it lit.

After taking a puff, he exhaled in bliss as he looked at the cig between his fingers with adoring eyes. Hoisting it to my face he offered me a drag. I refused for what seems now like a petty reason, prompting Vik to ask, "You don't like me very much, do you?"

Not wanting to admit my cast judgments, I stammered.

"It's not that… I just…"

"Don't worry I get it," he interjected my scramble for words.

"When I realized that I was bisexual, nothing about me changed. I was still the same person I was before my epiphany, but those that I told…the ones closest to me…they were the ones that changed. Everyone treated me differently, all except for Bell and Ellisia."

Feeling the shame of a person questioning their humanity, I felt the pain that flowed off Vik's words and the grief over the ones that walked out of his life.

Deciding to take him up on his offer for a drag of his cigarette, I touched his hand and peered into his mind. With his bags packed, he stood crying at his front door. Yelling, his mother tried to calm his father down as he shouted at Viktor to get the hell out of his house. Slamming the door in his face, his father continued his rant of ignorance.

"Bisexual means he's gay and I would die before saying I raised a gay son!"

His words echoed as I came to the present moment. Taking the cigarette, I brought it to my lips and pulled. Coughing my lungs out, it was apparent and no longer a secret that I had never smoked before. I only did it because after seeing what Vik endured and feeling how he felt, I understood. Everyone around him treated him differently just because he was being who he was—it prompted me then and there to vow that I would never contribute to that. I realized that the only reason I needed my shield of masculinity around him was because my masculinity itself was fragile.

When we headed back inside, we were both greeted by a wailing Bell who secretly drank our drinks while we were away. Switching chairs with Vik, Bell sat beside me as she failed to whisper softly in my ear.

"Don't tell her that I told you...but Ellisia over there still has her V card."

Overhearing her, she smacked Bell across her shoulder before receding into her chair and wallowing in embarrassment. Playing it off casually, I chuckled and changed the subject to spare Ellisia from Bell's loose tongue.

As the night aged, we made our way over to the dance floor and wedged ourselves between the bar and the blaring speakers. Pairing up with Ellisia, I realized that she was not much of a dancer, but Bell on the other hand, made her presence on the dancefloor known. Having an equally bold partner, she and Vik danced, wined, and drank till their heart's content.

Spending most of my time with Ellisia's supple ass gently grinding on my crotch to the beat of the music, I was often distracted by the way Bell move her hips and touched the floor as she writhed against Viktor.

Leaving her side, Vik ventured to the bar to get us drinks. Seeing that I had stopped on account of having to ride home safely, I was left with little to do as they drank. Asking Ellisia to cut in, Bell spun around and buried her small ass into my crotch as she moved to the song. A bit unsure and uncomfortable, my worried expression prompted Ellisia to laugh. Seeing Viktor as he approached made me instantly nervous. Glaring at him from behind his grinding girlfriend, he smiled and nodded. Feeling the ease of his approval, I indulged Bell in some sultry dancing as Vik and Ellisia engaged in some subtle grinding of their own.

It was a peculiar thing dancing with a woman and having her boyfriend right there, being okay with it. By the time we were ready to leave, I felt different about Ellisia and her pair of friends.

They were amazing people, and it was easy to quickly grow close to them all.

Walking out in our small group, we roamed the car park trying to find our vehicles. Not hard to miss, Bell's red Toyota Celica stood out with its low-slung frame and custom body modifications—all of which I was surprised to learn, she did herself. A fanatic when it came to cars, Bell considered herself a full-fledged gear head.

Announcing that the night was far from over, Vik told me to ride behind them as we made our way down the highway to Ellisia's apartment in California. Once we all got upstairs, Bell, Vik, and I sat in the living room while Ellisia fixed snacks in the kitchen. After fiddling in her purse for a few seconds, Bell revealed a lighter and something that looked like a cigarette. Running it under her nose, she inhaled deeply and gleefully sighed as if the smell had touched her soul.

"Sweet Mary Jane."

Seeing her lighter spit sparks, doused me with fearful paranoia. I knew if we got caught, we would have been in a heap of trouble.

Through My Eyes – The First Five

Taking her first drag, Bell blew her fumes upwards, filling the entire room with an earthy yet sweet smell. After another hit, she passed it to Viktor who enjoyed it even more than his cigarette. Given the pattern, I knew I was up next, but I had never done Mary Jane before. Up until that point, the only experiences I had with stuff like that were through my parents telling me to always say no.

The thing is, I did not know what I was saying no to. Having never tried it, I had no idea what it was like, how it tasted, how it felt nor if it was as bad as everyone said. Those questions were all I heard, and when it was my turn, I had a chance to give myself the answers, so I took it.

Taking a deep drag, I felt my lungs tighten as I coughed. With a surprised look on her face, Ellisia stared at the smoke rising from between my fingers before placing a tray of chips and cookies on the table in front of us. Knowing that it was logically her turn, I offered her a hit. Seemingly hesitant at first, she took it and inhaled deeply, coughing, and spewing smoke as she struggled. The glaring wide eyes of Viktor and Bell had me confused at first, but later that night Bell pulled me aside and told me that the only reason Ellisia smoked, was because I offered it to her, and that she had never done Mary Jane before.

Needing her to spell it out for me, she was a bit frustrated having to explain that Ellisia had a thing for me. Assuming I had known through her obvious signs, as a guy I was oblivious, thinking she was just a really kind and caring person.

Three hits were all it took to send me into a daze where time itself seemed to ripple as I moved. Colors were brighter and more appealing to the eyes—all sounds and smells drew my wandering attention. Every thought became a string of related ideas, each more inspiring than the last. Warm tingles flowed across my skin as even the simple act of touching something triggered seemingly foreign sensations. It was unlike anything I had ever experienced and the realm of thought that I was plunged into was wickedly seductive.

After mindlessly roaming my fields of thought for some time, I realized that Vik and Bell had vanished and Ellisia was curled up in a ball, asleep on the couch. Relieved of the warmth her fluffy hoodie provided, she shivered due to the lack of coverage of her black dress. Stumbling through her apartment, I ventured to her bedroom seeking a blanket. Opening the door, I was met by Vik and Bell.

With the back of her knees hanging off Viktor's arms, her hands were locked at the back of his head as he stood, holding her up. Thrusting his thick shaft into her hungry pussy, it took them a few seconds before noticing me.

Still in a haze, I wondered if what I was seeing was real or not. Before I could turn and walk away, Bell wailed, "No wait! … come inside and close the door."

Listening to her command, I looked to Viktor for some form of direction in the slowly rising awkwardness of the situation. Guiding me to Ellisia's desk chair, Bell sat me down and whispered in my ear.

"We like being watched."

Her words nursed an odd sensation that weaved itself through my body as it infected my thoughts. Seeing flashes of Bell in my head as she danced erotically on the dancefloor touching her body and grinding her hips, heavily contested my better judgment. The feeling of what I was doing was wrong...yet it added to the pleasures that made it feel so right.

With Viktor nodding in approval, his smile suggested he was more than happy to have me watch them as they fucked.

Spinning around, Bell gave me a clear view of her little ass as she walked over to Viktor and took to her knees. Squirming internally, I shifted in my chair as I adjusted to accommodate my growing erection. Not knowing my role in this rather peculiar situation, I was left with no other choice but to sit and enjoy the show.

Wrapping it with both hands, Bell hoisted Viktor's magnificent rod to her lips. Holding all eight inches between her fingers, she struggled to fit more than a couple inches of him past her small jaw. Eagerly she sucked and slobbered as she glazed his cock. Licking from his balls, she trailed his shaft with her tongue all the way to its pink head. Wrapping it in her lips, she worked her mouth as she stroked his dick, tracing along his chiselled stomach with her free hand. Thrilled by the sensation of her fingertips, he leaned his head back, took her head in his palm, and slowly began thrusting into her mouth. Gagging as her head bobbed back and forth, the ends of her hair bounced off her back while strings of saliva dripped from her lips to the floor.

The erotic sounds that flooded the room were enough to bring full strength to my erection as my cock fought angrily against my tented jeans. Resisting the urge to touch myself, I pleasured my eyes by looking on as Viktor bent Bell over at the edge of the bed.

Spreading her legs, he positioned himself behind her. With a tight grip, he pulled open her cheeks and fell to his knees. The sensation of his tongue sliding into her wet hole made her moan and sent a spasm down her legs. From where I sat, I heard the slushing sound of her pussy as he took her juices past his lips. Spread as wide as she could, Viktor held her snatch firmly against his face while the flicks of his tongue sent spasm after spasm rushing through her body. Clawing at the bedsheet, she bit into her bottom lip as the rising wave of her orgasm prepared to crash. Turning to me, the raw look in her eyes made my cock throb as she called out in blissful eroticism with her words hanging from her moans.

"Ohhh fuckkk…I'm cumming!"

Welcoming every drop of her orgasm into his mouth, the drips that escaped his lips slid down her quivering legs to her ankles.

Through My Eyes – The First Five

Spent, Bell fell onto the bed, revelling in her post-orgasmic heaven as Viktor took to his feet and stroked his thick staff of wonder. Moving in, he slid inch after inch of his rod into her slim frame, making it disappear into her wet pussy. As her hole was stretched and stuffed, she moaned, tugging at the sheets as her legs shook wildly.

Paying her no mercy, he fucked her with a flurry of long, deep strokes that made her cunt gleam a creamy white. In an orgasm-induced dazed, she mindlessly hung from the edge of the bed as Viktor pounded away at her flesh. Floating in the sea of an endless orgasm her gushing pussy pushed his cock from her hole as she squirted, soaking Ellisia's sheets.

Drained from her bouts of pleasure, she still listened when Viktor climbed onto the bed and ordered her to get on all fours. Sliding his rod back into her welcoming slit, her spent body happily accepted him with shudders of ecstasy. Locking eyes with me, she refused to leave my gaze as she was being fucked.

Awkwardly shifting in my seat, I sought the small release that came with the sensation of my cock rubbing against my jeans. Noticing my restlessness, they both stopped, got out of the bed, and walked over to me. Growing nervous as they approached, I had no idea what to expect when Bell slapped her hands against both armrests of my chair. Looking deep into my eyes, a moan ran past her bitten lip as Viktor took her from behind.

Dimitri Valentene

With each stroke into her drooling pussy, he thrusted harder and deeper as my chair shook with the rhythm of their pounding bodies. Her moans soon turned to shallow grunts as her cunt endured the stuffing of Viktor's eight-inch rod. Beads of sweat trailed her beautifully ample bouncing breasts as they dripped off her brown, pointed nipples and onto the crotch of my pants.

Mere inches from her swaying tits, her moans, and insistence on keeping eye contact made me feel like I was about to cum in my pants. Arching her back, she placed her hands on my thighs and her face firmly against my throbbing erection, giving me a clear view of Viktor demolishing her snatch. Looking up, I met his eyes as he stared at me with want and desire.

Surprised at first, I was more shocked to realize that it kind of turned me on. With each pump of his hips, he drove his cock into her pussy, slapping against her cheeks—each time, her face dragged along the shaft of my cock through my jeans. Falling prey to the sweet sensation of a pent-up release, I eased back into my seat as I felt my orgasm loom overhead. With his strokes quickening and the grunts he uttered, it was easy to tell that Vik was close too. Moaning to Bell that he was about to cum, I felt myself go past the point of no return. Shooting stream after stream of thick semen into my boxers, I felt the rush of ecstasy as her face continued to rub against me, milking every drop. Following my lead, Vik came, flooding Bell's hole as his seed dribbled out her gaping pussy and onto the floor.

After it was all over, we spent a few moments in exhaustive joy before they both headed into the shower to clean up. Still hooked in the sweet grips of Mary Jane, I remembered that Ellisia needed a blanket. Doing my best to process all that had just happened, my mind often fell to that look in Vik's eyes and the effect it had on me.

The questions it rose, I was in no state to answer so I simply attributed it to my wild night of drugs and alcohol.

After waiting for what seemed like forever for Bell and Viktor to finish up, I took a shower as I tried to wash off the heat of my most recent sin. When I got out, both Bell and Viktor were asleep in Ellisia's bed. I grabbed a pair of blankets and headed back to the living room. Draping the covers over Ellisia as she shivered, her jerks and partial words suggested she was having a nightmare.

While running the backs of my fingers along her cheek, I entered her mind out of curiosity, just to sneak a peek at what was upsetting her sleep. Seeing flashes, I heard the high revs of a motorcycle, followed by screeching tires and a loud bang. She was dreaming about her brother's crash. When I left her thoughts, I wanted to do something that would help without waking her up. Gently lifting her head, I rested it on my lap as I sat on the couch. Stroking her hair as I attempted to ease her turmoil, I thought about all the times that I was less than pleasant to her.

Knowing now what she had been through, and how she still managed to be as sweet and kind as she was towards me, made me feel like I was the world's worst person. My harsh self-analysis weighed heavy on my eyes, or maybe it was the M.J. —either way, I quickly fell asleep.

With Ellisia on my lap, and my head set firmly into the couch, we both slept soundly until morning came.

Chapter Twelve

B oth Ellisia and I awoke to the rather loud, erotic cries of profanities from Bell at the hands of Viktor.

"Good God, they're like rabbits!" she said as she rubbed the sleep from her eyes.

"How about we go get doubles or something?"

A masked attempt to escape the auditory assault.

In agreement, we hopped on Gabriella and rode to the nearest Doubles vendor. After receiving our order, we made our way over to the pavilion. Near the campus, it was a local drinking spot for students who wanted to listen to rather loud music from their cars.

Quiet, as it was a Saturday, Ellisia and I sat and ate, looking on as the wind rushed through the uncut grass.

"Are they always like that?"

The memories of last night's haze came forward.

"What do you mean always? Please don't tell me they made you watch!?"

She was clearly embarrassed.

"Well, last night you seemed cold, so I went looking for a blanket for you and...I kinda walked in on them. When Bell saw me, she made me stay. Do they always do things like this?"

"No, not with everyone, just the guys or girls they both find attractive."

A bit flattered that they both fancied me, I did my best to not let it go to my head.

"So...did you ever...you know...watch?" I awkwardly asked.

Almost choking on a sip of her drink, her cheeks immediately went red against her freckles as she wiped the spittle from her face. Seemingly fearful of judgment, she timidly answered.

"Maybe...Kinda...Okay I watched them once...just once I swear!" rambling on as if she was in trouble.

"You were never tempted to join them? They're your friends and after this morning, I'd say you guys are really close and comfortable—is it not your thing?"

My question made her think for a bit.

"It's not that. I'm still...well I've never done it with anyone before. After meeting Bell and Vik, people often think I'm as wild and willing as they are because we're friends. They may seem wild and out there, but they both really love each other. When Vik's dad put him out, Bell took him in and if it wasn't for Vik, Bell's ex would've eventually put her in the hospital. They fit well with each other, so they 'explore' with each other. I rather lose my V card to someone I love and can explore with, before joining one of their adventures. You know what mean?"

Bobbing my head in agreement, she drew my attention to two tiny spots of her thigh, her birthmarks. Being close together, they resembled snake bites.

"Watch this!"

She proceeded to make an imprint with her thumbnail.

"It's a smiley!" she happily exclaimed as I chuckled.

Talking for what felt like hours, the sun trailed across the sky as we moved from spot to spot, eventually ending up under a tree across the field.

"Darion...what's it like having your powers?"

113

Shocked, I had never been asked that before and never really thought about it. Scrambling my mind for an answer, my sense of urgency made me speak honestly, "It's tempting, fighting the urge to see into people's minds. With a single touch, I could tell what people are afraid of, the things that make them happy, even the things that turn them on. Lately, it's been a struggle trying to use it for the right things."

"Could you let someone into your mind? Like that day in class, when I touched your hand and saw your thoughts."

"That day was the first time it happened. I'm not sure if it would even work again."

"Could we try? Just once?"

Her pouting lips and puppy dog eyes made it impossible to say no. Initially, I should have thought it all through a bit better.

Giving her my palm, I focused on letting her in. When our fingers locked, she was pulled into my mind as random memories from my life flashed before her eyes. Unable to control the thoughts she saw, she played witness to fond family memories from before my parents' divorce.

Jumping ahead, she saw the many hours I worked on Gabriella, before she leapt into my memories of Space Night Club. Failing to stop her from what she was about to see, she was taken to the backseat of the car in Space's car park.

When I finally managed to push her out of my head, it was too late—she had seen and heard everything. She was hurt, and the look on her face could not have said it any louder. With welling tears, I saw the heartbreak in her eyes.

"Could we go home now?"

Obliging, we got on my bike and pulled up to her apartment building after a couple of minutes. Hopping off she started crying as she scampered up the stairs and into her bedroom. Following her, I called out in vain.

"Ellisia, wait! You weren't meant to see that! Would you please listen to me!?"

After slamming the door in my face, I was apprehended by a less than pleased Viktor and an angry Bell.

Not knowing how to explain my predicament without exposing my abilities, I asked them to apologize to Ellisia for me and tell her I would see her on Monday, before leaving and heading home.

On the ride and for the rest of my weekend, I often wondered why she got so upset. It was something that had happened long before I knew she even existed. Then it occurred to me— the look Ellisia had on her face when she saw my thoughts was no different from the one I had that day when I saw Miss Aly riding her husband in the car park.

Though I knew they were both different situations, it was obvious then how horrible the pain Ellisia had felt was, and though it was never my intention, I was the one who hurt her.

I had to right my wrongs, but I had no clue how to approach her to apologize. I thought about the possibility of her looking into my eyes and always seeing me and Ella—it made me feel a bit hollow thinking that she might never speak to me again.

Aside from a mountain of assignments, my weekend was filled with one failed idea after the other on how to properly make amends.

Chapter Thirteen

B y Monday morning, I still had nothing. Even as I hopped on Gabriella and rode to school, nothing came to mind—I was completely blank.

I opted for the good old heartfelt apology, hoping that it would be enough to at least get her to talk to me.

When I got to class and she finally walked in, she sat as far away from me as she possibly could. Throughout our lecture, I often stared at her, hoping that she would turn just long enough to see the sorrow in my eyes, but she never paid me a single glance.

After class I waited for her at the door, fidgeting with the straps of my book bag as I planned what I was going to say, praying that I don't mess up. Turning the corner, I wasted no time when I saw her.

"Hey…could we talk for a bit?"

By taking the stairs that led us to the gym at the end of the building, we were allowed some privacy.

"I'm sorry about what you saw. You have to believe me, I never wanted you to see that, and I really didn't want to hurt you, Ellisia. It's just, I never let anyone inside my thoughts before you…I couldn't control it."

With her face unphased as I spoke, I was unsure if I was getting through to her or not.

"I'm truly sorry…but if you never want to speak to me again, I'd understand."

Turning and walking off, I made it a few feet before she called out.

"Come by my apartment later…if you can."

Not knowing if I was forgiven or not, I was sure about one thing—nothing was going to keep me from seeing her after school.

Vanishing after our morning class, some of her friends on campus said that she went home for the day. A bit concerned, I knew I would be seeing her in a bit, so I thought it best to just make good notes and take them to her. When class finally ended, I was the first one out the door and in the carpark.

As Gabriella growled and purred to life, I made my way out the gates and to the backroads of California. When I got there, her front door was unlocked so I announced myself and stepped in.

"In here…"

Ellisia's voice called from the bedroom.

Knocking first, I was met with, "No need to knock, just come in."

Befuddled, I walked into what seemed like an empty room. Taking a few steps, I called out, "Ellisia, you here?" only to be startled by the door slamming shut behind me.

When I spun around, I was lost for words. In a fitted white top, she revealed what little cleavage she had as a pair of black jeans lovingly hugged her curvaceous thighs and ample ass, rounding the look off with a pair of red, strapped heels. She looked exactly like Ella did that night at the club.

Before I could begin to process my thoughts to even speak, Ellisia stepped towards me.

"Get on your knees!"

Admittingly, even though the demanding persona she tried to project did not suit her, I felt a shudder of weakness in my stomach that made me want to comply. Fighting the urge to be ordered around and taken advantage of, I decided on being a decent person at that moment and denied my desire.

"Ell…isia…"

I fumbled her name with Ella's.

"I know for a fact, that this isn't you. These clothes, those shoes, I could tell by your face alone how uncomfortable you are. Why are you doing all this?"

Angrily exhaling, she ground her teeth and glared at me with teary eyes and clenched brow. Shoving me aside, she made her way over to the edge of the bed before she broke down crying. Gravitating towards the distressed damsel, I sat beside her and remained silent. Eventually, she spoke through her sobs.

"I like you…I really like you Darion. Ever since the first day of class—even after you were so rude and pig-headed. I've been sad for a long time, but somehow whenever I'm around you…it doesn't feel as bad. You make it feel like he's not really gone. I wanted you to like me back, but after I saw the memories with you and Ella, I knew I was nothing like her. I figured if I dressed like this and acted how she acted, you would have at least given me a chance."

Touched by the lengths she had gone, I smiled.

"You don't have to be like Ella for me to like you. I already like you just the way you are."

"You like me?" she asked as the raising hope became audible in her voice.

"I do. If I'm being honest, when I'm around you, I often forget the things that trouble me. Somehow, it all seems to fade away when we're together. So you see, you don't need to be like her, just be you. It's hard not to like you, especially with your adorable freckles."

With her cheeks cast red, she blushed and sighed a happy sigh.

"Wanna stay late and watch a movie?"

I nodded with a smile.

Almost four years old at the time, we watched Nick and Norah's Infinite Playlist. Never having seen it before, she assured me that it was a great movie. Huddled up on her couch, we sat under dimmed lights with bowls of popcorn, chips, and cookies on the table in front of us.

After a few minutes in, I was hooked. The movie was unexpectedly interesting and had a lot of soundtracks that appealed to my taste.

With her wrapped in my arm as we watched, a rather heated scene started unfolding on screen. Our eyes were glued to the TV, looking on as Nick descended Norah's body with his lips. Ellisia's breathing got heavier. Moving and shifting, she did her best to accommodate the obvious heat that had set in between her legs. By the time Norah had her orgasm in the movie, she was flushed—her petite bosom heaved with her breaths.

From the corner of my eyes, I saw her staring up at me. When I turned to look, she lifted and stole a kiss. Hooked by the sudden sensation of her soft lips, I ran my fingers through her hair and kissed her back. It felt amazing and neither of us wanted to stop, getting more intense with every second that passed us by. Making her way onto my lap, she was still wearing her fitted white top but swapped her jeans out for a pair of shorts that joyfully accommodated curious fingers.

Her once stolen peck quickly grew to locked tongues, bitten lips, and sweet moans that came from the sensations of each other's flesh. Sliding my hands further up her shorts, I gripped handfuls of her soft, giving cheeks, which I noticed were also freckled. The feeling of her ass between my fingers was exquisitely erotic, driving wave after wave of raw desire through every fiber of my being.

Spreading her ass as we kissed pushed a whimper past her lips. Her wandering fingers worked through my hair as she took a moment to look at me—eyes alight with a fiery yearning. From my lips to my cheek then to my neck, she placed her trail of kisses before gently biting. As her teeth brushed against my skin, my budding erection throbbed. Wedged between her legs, it pressed firmly against her pussy, growing with the subtle strokes of her gently grinding hips.

Still fondling her ass, I eventually convinced myself to let go of her seductive flesh. Sliding upwards, I worked my hands under the waistband of her shorts, causing them to ride up. With most of her butt now out, her shorts gently wedged itself between her cheeks and the slit of her pussy. Though she was not exposed, her camel toe left little to the imagination.

With furious fingers, she undid my belt and unbuttoned my jeans. Sliding my zipper down, she exposed the bulge of my hard cock through my boxers. Leaving them on, she sat on me and began slowly working her hips. With my cock sitting between the luscious lips of her pussy, she rubbed her clit along my shaft. As we kissed in between the moans and heat of our griding bodies, I felt a warm wetness slowly engulf my throbbing cock. Near dripping wet, Ellisia soaked through both her underwear and shorts. Seeping into my boxers, her juices lubed my dick as she grinded harder. Her moans turned to grunts as she bore down with all her desire onto my staff and worked herself to a climax.

Feeling the pressure of my approaching orgasm, the way Ellisa bit her lip and spasmed, I knew she too was about to cum. Doing my best to hold off until I heard her say those magical words, I erupted the moment they slipped past her lips.

"Fuck…I'm cumming…hmmm I'm cumming… fuck fuck fuckkkkk…"

She screamed in ecstasy.

Falling into my chest, her pussy spilled its sweet nectar as I shot ropes of cum that pooled in my boxers. Locked in her arms, her grinding hips slowed to a stop as we both noted the sticky mess between us but preferred to revel in our orgasmic exhaustion a bit longer.

After we ended our sultry act and washed up, Ellisia asked if I wanted to spend the night. Given how looking at a movie ended, most would assume we spent the rest of the night committing equally erotic sins, but instead, we laid up in her bed and talked until we saw the sun peeking through her windows.

Though she did make attempts, I told her that given how she felt earlier, she should wait until she was sure that I was the one she wanted as her first. It just didn't feel right, and I did not want her bearing the pain of a regretful first time. I knew all too well what that felt like now.

Agreeing with me, it did not stop us from dry humping each other to two more body quivering orgasms during our long conversation.

Chapter Fourteen

Over the coming months, Ellisia and I were near inseparable. Spending all day at each other's side during classes, I stayed the night at her apartment at least four times a week. Never having sex, we often stripped down to our underwear and writhe against each other's bodies until we orgasmed, in attempts to satisfy our urges. We did our best to avoid the temptation of oral sex because let's face it, it was a way too easy transition to penetration, and I rather wait for Ellisia to say when she's ready.

The more time we spent together, the stronger my feelings got as I often practiced letting her into my mind. It took a bit of time to get it right, but I was able to let her into my thoughts and show her specific memories with a single touch. She was an amazing girl, once you took the time to get to know her. She was intelligent, fun-loving, and extremely determined to exceed in her field, often helping me with assignments and group projects. She preferred dogs to cats but loved them both, her favorite colors were blue, purple, and pink, and she had an unusual fear of birds. What surprised me the most was that she was, in secret, somewhat of a weeb. Though her apartment never showed it, her room back home was filled with pictures and plushies of characters from Naruto—someone named Kakashi in particular.

I never fancied anime, but Ellisia did and given how many times she opted for us to watch the series after she had told me her 'secret', I thought it best to learn more so we could talk about it. At first, it was work but I too fell in love with the amazing Japanese cartoon and we even bought a decal of the Hidden Leaf symbol for Gabriella.

Our weekends were always dedicated to spending time with Vik and Bell—this gave the four of us a chance to get closer. Soon the Three Musketeers became the Fantastic Four, and I had found a group of rather colourful friends.

With a little convincing from Ellisia, I told them both my secret, but they were not convinced until I gave them a demonstration of my abilities. Promising never to speak a word about it to anyone, I knew they were both trustworthy people—after all, I had seen into their minds. When they realized I was not lying, they had more than a few questions that took hours to answer. They went back and forth asking what does it feel like, could I see things people didn't know existed in their own minds, have I ever met anyone like me, and on and on they went till the early hours of the morning.

Between Bell and Vik, I was closer to Bell seeing that she and I had a bit more in common. She loved cars and I loved motorcycles. She often let me work on Gabriella at her uncle's garage, offering help whenever I needed it. We had a lot to talk about, and with Vik and Ellisia at our sides, we attended many car and bike shows. Oddly enough, we were often left alone as our significant others wandered off in boredom.

The friendship between Vik and I changed nearing the end of my first semester. It was a few weeks before final exams and Vik's nineteenth birthday was right around the corner. Agreeing to all meet at Bell's uncle's garage first, when Ellisia and I pulled up, she was preoccupied with a customer's car. Having to get it fixed before we all left for a night out, she was having an array of issues with the alternator. When the birthday boy finally arrived, he was in a less than happy mood. This only got worse with Bell's realization that it would take her a couple more hours to fix the car.

Seeing someone sad on their birthday always felt disheartening to me—I believed that if there was one day every year that you should truly be happy was on your birthday.

Pulling Ellisia aside, I told her what I intended to do. After she agreed, I handed Viktor her helmet.

127

Dimitri Valentene

"Here Vik, put this on, let's go for a ride. Ellisia would stay here with Bell and when they're done, they'd come meet us."

"You sure? You don't want to take Bell's car instead?"

"I'm sure buddy, plus neither of them could work Gabriella—she's a bit peculiar. Just hop on, we'd go to The Rise."

Unsure of what to do with his hands once he sat behind me, I took them and wrapped them around my waist, and told him to hold on. Admittingly, it did feel weird at first, but Vik was my friend, and no strain of friable masculinity was enough to change that.

When we got there and finally parked, we took a table outside so that we would see when the girls arrived, plus it was quiet enough to talk and Viktor could smoke freely. It took a little while to get our drink after placing our order, as usual, the place was packed.

"What's bothering you?" I asked as he lit his second cigarette in ten minutes.

"Is it that obvious?"

He took a drag.

"I went to visit my parents today. Mom was happy to see me, she gave me a tight hug and a kiss, wishing me a happy birthday as any good mother would. But my dad...he refused to let me inside the house."

Speaking in between sips of his beer, Vik told me more about his family.

"It was great in the beginning before I realized I liked guys too. My dad and I were a lot closer back then. He taught me everything—how to ride a bike, how to shave, how to drive, and even how to talk to girls. But the day I told them, he changed the instant I spoke those words. He stopped caring almost immediately—it truly did feel like was no longer his son. Sometimes, just sometimes, I wish I could go back and change that one thing."

"Why?" I interjected. "Why would you do that to yourself? You rather deny who you are, solely for the purpose of pleasing your father? Vik, it sounds like your mom loves you regardless of your preferences so your dad could do the same. You're not the problem here, he is. You need to see that."

"I know…it's just, what if he never accepts me?"

His head hung in the sadness of his thoughts.

"Well, honestly Vik, he would be missing out on getting to know a really great guy." Lifting my bottle, I cheered, "Happy birthday buddy!"

Finally coaxing a smile out of him, I asked a bold question hoping to change the subject to a more uplifting one.

"Sooo…what's it like…you know…being with a guy?"

129

Momentarily stunned by my question, he quickly cracked a sneaky smile and extended his hand.

"See for yourself."

Hesitant, I wondered if I was ready for what I was about to see. I tried my best to brace myself for the wildness of his sexcapades by taking a deep breath and mentally preparing before grabbing hold of his hand. Not wanting to jump into the deep end, I dove into one of his memories that included Bell.

Taken to the bedroom of their apartment, Viktor was standing while Bell and a male friend were on their knees in front of him. Kissing and swirling their tongues over the head of his cock, they took turns throating his shaft. Their male companion was around the same height as Bell. With a slim waist and wide hips for a guy, he had a strikingly feminine figure. Oddly enough his ass was fuller and more supple than Bell's, hypnotically jiggling as he trotted.

Taking to her feet, Bell rummaged through their nightstand, pulled out a bottle of lube before handing it to Vik, and made her way over to a couch that faced the bed. After sitting, she lifted her legs and hung them over each armrest. Spread wide, she gave both men a clear view of her wet pussy as she watched them and finger fucked herself.

Guiding him to the bed, Viktor made his friend bend over and get on all fours. Tearing the condom wrapper open with his teeth, he slid its latex along his rod before slathering and stroking it with lube. Dripping some on the guy's hole, he circled it with his finger before sliding it in. When he did, I heard the most sultry, male grunt escape the man's lips. Followed by Vik's meaty staff, I heard him moan out as inch after inch slid into his ass and stretched his hole. When Viktor was all in, I saw his friend's legs shudder as a clear liquid drooled from the tip of his limp penis.

"Fuck me harder!" he moaed as he called Viktor daddy—the sound of pounding flesh was accompanied by his uninhibited wails of pleasure.

It was strange seeing a man act that way during sex.

The faster Vik fucked his ass, the louder he moaned and the more clear liquid drooled from his dick, pooling on the bed. With a few rather soulful grunts, he tensed up as the dripping liquid was replaced by streams of spurting cum. I was astonished to see a man ejaculate like that. Seeing the way Viktor dominated his friend filled my head with odd questions. Before I knew it, I was aroused and wondering about the pleasures his friend experienced. When I stepped out of his mind, I had a growing erection and an assortment of contradictory thoughts.

Doing my best to play it off, when I came out of his mind, I slid back into my seat and all I could have said was, "I see," knowing then and there that it rose feelings and questions that would linger in my head.

I was unsure, but I felt like there were parts of me that would have enjoyed being Vik's friend in that situation.

As an awkward silence set in, Vik attempted to change the topic yet again, hoping to cut the newfound tension.

"So how long have you had Gabbi?"

"Gabbi? Oh you're talking about Gabriella…urm… a little more than a year now. I bought her from some guy who was more than happy to part ways with her, don't know why. Once I fixed her up and gave her some love, she was tearing up the asphalt like the iron goddess she was meant to be."

"Hmmm, it makes sense now. I know why Elli likes you, but now I see why you like her."

A bit confused as to how we jumped from Gabriella to Ellisia, the bewildered look on my face prompted him to explain, with a question of all things.

"Why did you pick her? Out of all the running bikes for that price, why did you pick Gabriella?"

"I don't know. When I saw her, she was half-covered and a bit weathered. She was still in decent condition—I knew I could save her if I put in the wrench time. I guess I found the idea of fixing her up appealing."

"You like fixing things… Only broken things need fixing, and you and I both know that even though she doesn't show it as much, Elli is broken."

132

A bit insulted by his assumption, he quickly explained he was not trying to offend.

"It's a good thing, don't misunderstand me. I see the love and care you give to your bike—it tells me that you'd give even more love and affection to Elli and that's what's important to me."

Vik was a bit too insightful for his own good at times. His words made me think—they made me remember.

My feelings for Ella started when I had seen her pain—when I saw she was broken. Seeing that she needed someone, made me want to be that someone. Vik was right, I was attracted to broken people and driven by an urge to help them pick up the pieces. I felt like there was a revelation to be made but before I could dive too deep in thought, Bell called Viktor and told him that we should come back—she won't be able to finish the car in time. A bit saddened that we had to leave, I turned to Vik…

"Sorry buddy, really wished your birthday wasn't so dull."

"Nah man, it's fine, plus this was fun. Short but fun, thank you."

Sharing a smile, we dawned our helmets and rode back to the garage. When we got there, it took Bell until after midnight to get the car running. Not wanting Vik's birthday to be a bust, we ordered pizza, got snacks, some Mary Jane, and headed to Ellisia's apartment.

Chapter Fifteen
Lessons In Lust

Bell started smoking moments before entering the apartment, saying that she needed some stress relief. Passing it around, we all took a couple of drags and were eagerly awaiting the pizza delivery guy. Famished because of the munchies, we rushed the pizza when it came and sent the delivery guy on his way with a generous tip. Too engrossed in eating to make conversation, we all had somehow forgotten how incredible pizza tasted. As our pangs of hunger were quelled, Bell offered an idea. Turning on some music, she played it just loud enough so that we could all hear before suggesting we played a game.

One of her own making, it was a mix of spin the bottle and truth or dare. We each took turns spinning the bottle—whoever it landed on had to choose either truth or dare. They could never choose the same option twice in a row. This meant if you chose truth, and the bottle landed on you a second time, you had to choose dare.

After a few rounds of trivial truths and less than daring dares, Bell, being the person that she was, went from zero to ten in an instant. With the bottle landing on me and my luck being how it was, I had one option— dare. Giving the appearance of contemplation, she tapped her finger against her chin.

"Hmmm…Darion, I dare you to kiss Viktor."

"Bell!" Ellisia shouted in protest, "why would you dare him to do something like that? I told you he's not into that!"

Stunned by her point of issue, I was more concerned about the fact that they were friends, and I did not want to cause any problems. Oddly, I was not against the idea of kissing Vik. Until that point, I had never thought about it, and when Bell brought it up, I didn't shudder at the idea like I thought I would have.

"It's okay Ellisia, I don't think I mind it," bringing an end to her protest.

"You sure hun…you really don't have to listen to Bell."

"It's fine, it'll be a learning experience plus… I kinda want to."

As the tension settled amongst us, a new tension reared its head as I signaled Vik to lean in. When our lips met and we finally kissed, it was just that, a kiss. Though it was a great kiss, it was not as weird as I thought it would have been—in fact, it was rather pleasant. His lips were soft, and he was a good kisser—plus it seemed to turn Bell on while casting Ellisia's freckled cheeks red.

When it was Vik's turn and he spun the bottle, it landed on Bell. Having to choose truth, Viktor looked at Bell and smiled.

"Besides yours truly, who else in this room would you sleep with?"

Without wasting a breath, she responded near-instantly.

"That's an easy one, both of them!"

With Ellisia unphased by Bell's answer, I was unable to hide my smile and subtle blushes. Luckily when it came to her friends, Ellisia was very understanding and trusting of Bell and Vik.

It never struck me as such at first, but what the four of us shared was different—it was special.

Next was my turn, and to my joy, it landed on Bell. Already knowing she had to pick dare, I spoke before the bottle completely settled.

"Bell, I dare you to kiss Ellisia."

I was expecting hesitation or a protesting reaction, but again it was Bell. Leaning across our little circle, she yanked Ellisia in and enthusiastically locked lips. Adding her personal touch, she ran her fingers through Ellisia's hair, nibbled and bit her lips, and stuck her tongue in her throat.

When she had finished, Ellisia was flushed—with heavy breaths she signalled her arousal. Shamelessly, Vik and I were also turned on by the whole thing, a fact we displayed unknowingly through our tented jeans. In unison, the three of us adjusted ourselves before we continued, thanks to Bell. Finally, it was Ellisia's turn. With the bottle landing on me, I had to choose truth, which prompted her question.

"Where did you lose your virginity?"

Hesitant, I contemplated for a bit before deciding to tell them.

"I lost it when I was in high school,"

My proclamation prompted Bell to call me an early bloomer as Vik laughed.

"I lost my virginity to my Math teacher," I said, creating a deafening silence throughout the room.

"Wait…what? A teacher? How old were you? How old was she? Or he?"

Bell's sudden change in tone demanded I answer.

"Firstly, it was a woman and secondly I was eighteen, so it was okay," I rebutted as I defended myself.

Pausing our game, they insisted I tell them about Miss Alysandra. Seeing that they were my friends, I gave them the entire story—beginning to end. When it was over and I told them how we had parted ways, Bell's eyes were filled with tears. Knowing she always did her best to appear rough and tough, her watery eyes were cause for alarm. Leaning in she hugged me tightly as I remained stiff in befuddlement.

Whispering, she told me, "I know what it's like loving someone like that."

Before I could respond, Vik's hand on my shoulder pulled my attention.

"Dude, it really sounds like you were taken advantage of. From what you said, you and Alysandra never really spoke…it was just about the sex. She used you man…and then left you in pieces. It doesn't matter if you were eighteen or not, she was wrong for what she did."

The more they spoke, the more I came to realize they could be right. I was no longer looking at my first sexual relationship the same way. Instead, I struggled to discern if what had happened with Miss Aly was even consensual.

Thinking back, she never asked me anything, she just led and as her student, I followed.

"Was I really taken advantage of, or did I want it? It felt like I wanted it…I knew I wanted it…did I really want it?"

Distracted by my thoughts, I took to my feet.

"Guys, I think I need to be alone for a bit."

Making my way to Ellisia's bedroom, I shut the door behind me, sat at the edge of the bed, and let my sea of questions consume me. Growing to near-deafening volumes in my head, the noise shattered about ten minutes later when Ellisia came knocking on the door. Stepping in, she immediately apologized.

"Sorry about my question, I wouldn't have asked it if I knew it would have bothered you this much."

"It's not your fault. You, Vik, and Bell were right, I was taken advantage of. The thing is, I don't know how I'm supposed to feel about that. As a guy, I should be thrilled, right? Is something wrong with me?"

"Nothing is wrong with you Darion. It's just with guys…with guys sex is taught to be an accomplishment. Even when a man is taken advantage of, especially by a woman, he's taught to view it as a good thing, as an achievement. Nothing is wrong with you—it's sad how the world is."

Not knowing that tears were flowing from my eyes, I was confused when they fell from my cheeks as I was not crying. Yet, for some reason, they just poured.

"How should I feel now?"

I was unsure how to properly process my realizations.

"Whatever comes we'd face it, and we'd deal with it…together."

Taking my hand and holding it tightly in hers, she did her best to comfort me.

Chapter Sixteen

Leaning in, she placed a soft kiss against my lips. Gentle at first, they grew more intense as I played along—soon I got caught up in the heat of the moment myself. Pushing me back into the bed, she placed her glorious cheeks on my crotch and continued kissing. Piece by piece, we relieved each other of our clothes as we stripped to our underwear. With straying hands, she took hold of the elastic of my boxers and attempted to slide them down. Holding her wrists, I stopped her and pulled her into me before rolling over.

"You sure you're ready?"

She replied with eager eyes and a simple bob of the head. Locking lips, I explored her body with my hands, squeezing the sensuous flesh of her breasts and stomach as I caressed her many curves with my fingertips.

Sliding my hand beneath the white lace of her panties, she gasped at the sensation of my finger gently brushing her clit. Hearing her subtle breaths grow heavier in my ear, I explored the slit of her honey hole, trailing her juices up and down while smearing it on her puffy lips as I worked her pussy. Slowly I inched it into her wet hole, admiring the ways her toes curled and stretched as her walls rubbed against my finger. Sliding back and forth, I fingered her as I kissed her lips and licked her neck. Stopping for a moment to pull out of her hole, I brought my finger to my lips, looked her in the eyes, and licked her sweet nectar off it. Her eyes were ablaze with fiery lust and a deep yearning. Taking my hand, she tasted herself before sliding it back between her legs.

"Use two fingers this time."

Following her request, I ran two of my fingers between the lips of her pussy. Occasionally moving a bit upwards and teasing her clit, her juices lubed my fingers enough to slide inside. Taking it slowly, her wet pussy gripped my fingers and squeezed them together as I made my way deeper into her.

Once at the knuckle, I gently moved back and forth. Driving spasms down her legs and moans past her lips, her pussy got wetter, and I was able to freely fuck her with my fingers. With her orgasm on the rise, I continued to work her cunt with my hand until she groaned and moaned out.

Without warning, I felt her hole tense up as a warmth rushed along my fingers and into my palm. Having came, her body twitched as her toes curled and she uttered her final moans.

Enduring the last moments of her fading orgasm, I made my way down her body with my tender lips and curious tongue. Paying her small boobs ample attention, I covered her hard, dark brown nipples with my lips and showered them with a flurry of flicks from my tongue. Captivated by her—the smell of her skin, the sounds of her moans, and the sensations of her touch were enough to send pulses through my already hard cock. Proudly tenting my boxers, its eagerness left a small, wet spot of precum on my shorts.

Kissing along her stomach, I nibbled and licked its sinuous flesh before making my way over her mound. Removing her laced underwear, I was met by a pair of voluptuous pussy lips and her sacred honey dribbling out of her hole, making for a mouth-watering sight. Prepping my lips with a good lick, I leaned in as I noticed her lack of smell. Burying my face between her legs, I kissed her snatch and licked off her spilled juices.

"Fuck that feels good." She moaned as she experienced a tongue between her legs for the first time.

After teasing her clit and seeing her body writhe and twist in pure anticipation, I stopped.

"Bend over at the edge of the bed."

I made my way to my feet.

143

Doing as she was told, Ellisia arched her back and hoisted her glorious ass as her cheeks jiggled. With her face pressed against a pillow, I dropped to my knees behind her.

"Spread your cheeks."

"Urm…okay…"

She seemed a bit unsure as to what was about to happen.

With a clear view of both her holes, I snuggled my face between her open crack and rimmed her ass with my tongue. Pulling away from my face, I was prompted to ask, "Is everything okay? Do you not like that? Want me to stop?"

"God no, don't stop, it just felt different that's all."

Pushing back into my face, I happily resumed eating her ass from behind as my prodding tongue slid into her bum. With pointed toes, she pulled at the sheets and moaned while my tongue joyously danced from her pussy to her butt hole. Her taste was intoxicating, and her sultry cries of pleasure provided all the encouragement I needed to drive my face deeper into her nether region.

Using my thumb, I parted her slit and slowly slid it into her welcoming hole while my tongue deeply explored her backdoor. With my entire thumb finally in, I pressed down against her walls and massaged her clit with my index finger.

Through My Eyes – The First Five

"Hmmmm…Mhhhhh…yesssss just like that! Fuuuuuckkkkk… that feelsss soooooo fucking gooooddd! Don't stoppp pleaseeee!"

Her thighs trembled as her pointed toes curled in.

From her moans, I could tell that she had bitten on her pillow as she prepared for a soul-shaking orgasm. Her fingers wove through the sheets, her tightening grip yanking it from its corners as I tongued her ass and fingered her cunt. All the waves of pleasure that riddled her body made her wetter, filling the room with the lewd slushing sounds of her holes.

Releasing the pillow from between her teeth, she called out with a high-pitched voice as her cries melded with her moans.

"I'mm cuminnggg again…Ahhhhhh!"

While doing my best to continue working her as she came, the crashing wave of her orgasm caused her spasming pussy to gush. Blasting my face as she squirted, she fell forward into the arms of her climax. Covered by the gleaming trails and beads of her ejaculation, I licked her off my hand and noted the almost sweet taste as it coated my tongue and slid to the back of my throat.

She tasted exquisite.

When I stood up, she crawled to the edge of the bed and sat. With her face mere inches from my concealed erection, I felt the heat of her breath seep through the fabric of my boxers. Looking up at me with wide, innocent eyes, her roaming hands slid my boxer shorts down my thighs. Springing up when relieved of its prison, the head of my dick brushed against her lips as if it was eager to introduce itself. Unsure of exactly what to do, she took my shaft in her hand and stroked as if she was scared that she would break it.

"You could move your hands faster you know, you won't hurt me, so don't worry."

Quickening her pace, she stroked my cock a bit harder than before.

"Like this?" she asked as I replied with a breathy, "Mmmhmm," while rocking my head back in bliss.

I felt a slight buckle in my knees as the feeling of her warm tongue dragged along the length of my rod and swirled the precum at my head. Sadly, her range of know-how ended there.

Not knowing how to properly suck a cock, I felt more than a couple teeth that made me wince. Embarrassed by my flinches, she pulled my dick from her mouth as strings of her saliva stretched from her lips.

"I'm sorry...I'd stop if it's that bad," she said with an apologetic ring to her voice.

"It's not that it's bad... your mouth feels great...it's just... your teeth. It really hurts when they...you know...rub against it while you suck."

"Is it okay if I try again?" she asked innocently.

Through My Eyes – The First Five

"Sure," I said with a smile, secretly bracing myself.

I guess I had become a sucker for her bright eyes and cute voice to be willing to endure the sharp brushes of teeth as she figured it all out.

A few failed attempts later, I realized I had to switch it up a bit if I wanted to avoid the occasional stabs of pain. With my palm, I took her chin and leaned in to meet her wet lips. Putting every ounce of my emotions into a single kiss, I passed them along through the tip of my tongue as it frolicked with hers.

"Lean back."

I hoisted her smooth, curvaceous legs, tracing the tender skin of her calves with moist kisses. Bringing her french-tipped toenails to my face, I dragged my lips along her ankles, licking her insteps before nibbling on each of her toes. Sticking my cock between her thick thighs, it rested on the mound of her pussy, just barely rubbing against her wet clit. While my lips admired her precious feet, I moved my hips back and forth, fucking her thighs and rubbing her clit with every thrust.

Taking a moment, I fished my wallet from my jeans and took out a condom from one of the slots.

"No…no condoms, not for my first time. I wanna feel everything."

She took the square packet from my hand and pulled me up onto the bed. With us now face to face, I

147

looked into her eyes—they were filled with desire and a bit of fear.

"Ready?"

"Mmmm hmmm," she hummed and nodded.

"If it hurts too much, let me know and I'd stop, okay?"

"Okay...wait, if it's not too weird... do you mind wearing something for me?"

Curious as to what she could possibly want me to put on at a time like this, her kinkiness reared its head as she pulled a blue ninja headband from her nightstand, along with a tiny bottle of lube. Seeing the symbol engraved on the metal plate of the headband, I instantly knew where it was from. Not wanting to say no and possibly ruin the mood, I agreed and tied it around my forehead, which seemed to turn her on a bit more.

"Like this?"

"Yessss, now that's sexy!"

Using the lube, I dripped it onto the head of my dick and stroked it along the shaft until its entirety glistened against the light of the bedroom. After finding a comfortable angle, I lined up the head of my throbbing cock with her slippery slit and gently applied pressure. With less than an inch in, she winced and groaned as the pain set it. Her hole was incredibly tight, even when fully lubed, the walls of her pussy felt like a vice on my shaft.

Through My Eyes – The First Five

"You're okay, right? If you want me to stop at any time, just tell me,"

Her face bore the looks of pain.

"No, don't stop…it hurts, but I don't want you to stop."

Spreading her legs wider, I slowly pushed more of my rod into her pussy until she had taken most of it.

Yanking me into her arms, her lips rested near my ear.

"Take me," she uttered amidst her moans and groans.

With a less than gentle thrust, I shoved the last half inch of my dick into her stretching cunt—a loud moan breached her lips. With all of me inside her, her pussy fitted like a finely tailored glove, gripping my shaft as I moved my hips.

With slow, short strokes, I enjoyed the warmth of her honey hole as her gasps became moans. Weaving my fingers between hers, I pinned her hands to the bed as I gradually quickened the pace of my hips. With the waves of her wetness trickling out of her busy pussy, I felt my cock slide in and out more freely.

"Fuck me!" She loosened the knots of our fingers and wrapped her hands around my back.

Clamping me with her legs, the heat of our bodies melded as she begged again.

"Please… fuck me!"

Slow strokes grew to the loud, lewd slapping of flesh while beads of sweat dripped from my brow. With each pump into her snatch, I felt the heat spread from my loins throughout my body as my orgasm encroached. No longer moaning, soulful grunts and wails slipped beyond her lips as I buried my cock between her legs. Drawing my eyes, she looked into them and announced her incoming release.

"Babe…I think I'm gonna cum again."

Attempting to fuck her through her orgasm, her tightening hole and spasming legs as she came brought me to my climax. Sinking her nails into my back, she clawed at my skin as she orgasmed and I filled her hole with beads of thick, sticky cum.

Rolling her over, she lay in my arms as we both struggled to catch our breaths. Speaking in unison, we both exclaimed, "That was fucking amazing!"

With a kiss, Ellisia smiled and said, "I love you."

Sure that I felt the same way about her, I held her tightly in my arms and whispered, "I love you too…Elli."

Forgetting that Bell and Vik were still in the apartment, we rushed to get dressed and head to the living room. When we stepped out the door, we were…more like *Ellisia* was given a round of applause.

Having heard most of our romp, they both congratulated an embarrassed Elli for finally losing her virginity.

Chapter Seventeen

After that night, Elli took her first morning-after pill that she got from Bell. Making it a priority to always have condoms on me, there were more than a few times where the heat of the moment didn't allow it.

Her first time started a wild train ride of sexual adventures over the next few months. Her appetite was near insatiable as she grabbed and groped my crotch the moment no one was looking. We had sex every night, and every morning before classes, yet by lunch, she would be sucking my cock and stuffing it up her pussy in the handicap stall of the student washroom.

Through My Eyes – The First Five

We had sex every single time she was horny—it seemed like she had no control over her desire. I had no issue whatsoever—I was simply glad to be the one she was desiring.

She soon got a bit bolder and more public. Leaving the comfort of fucking in random classrooms of the new building, we often had quickies in the campus carpark, hand jobs in the library, and full-on sex sessions in the restrooms of the few bars and restaurants that were near the university.

Bit by bit she also let me in on her many fetishes which revolved heavily around cosplay in the bedroom. There was one time that she referred to me as 'Hokage' the entire time we were being intimate.

In all honesty, it was a bit weird, but whenever she made me dress up, the sex would be mind-blowingly animalistic. She would change from this meek, soft-spoken girl to a raging, cock-craving vixen that made my knees weak with each magical flutter of her tongue. What surprised me most was how much she loved being called a slut behind closed doors. Simply whispering in her ear, "You're my little slut," was enough to moisten her panties and set the heat between her legs. I was perfectly happy being with her every day. Though we were mostly in school, it was always an amazing adventure of laughs, love, and risky sex.

Now, on our Friday night outings, both Elli and I had sultry tales to share at the bar with Vik and Bell.

On the day of our last exam, I was sadly informed that I was unable to sit through the test seeing that I had failed the coursework for the term. Taking the news as anyone would, I felt a deep sinking feeling in my gut as I imagined the various ways my life would hit a dead end due to that one failed course. Luckily my lecturer offered me a solution—I could simply retake the course with the part-time class next semester, and it should not affect the rest of my classes.

Giving Elli a kiss good luck, I told her that I would meet her at the apartment later to celebrate exams finally being over. Having some time alone, I decided to take Gabriella to Bell's garage seeing that she and Vik were off for the week in preparation for their final exams. With a short ten-minute ride, I pulled into the car park. When I got inside, it was void of life—some tools we scattered about, and the hood of a Nissan was still popped open as if someone had been working on it recently.

"Vik!... Bell!... You guys here?"

I lifted my visor, hoping to get an answer.

Through my calls, a muffled scream briefly echoed from behind the garage that drew me in like a witless moth to an open flame.

When I closed in on the washrooms at the back of the building, some guy had Bell pinned to the wall with his hand over her mouth—it was her ex-boyfriend. I try not to think about what he was about to do or what would have happened to Bell if I hadn't shown up. God alone knows his intention was less than humane.

He was near twice my size…if I had mindlessly rushed in, he would have easily put me on my ass. I was terrified, but I was not about to let my friend become another statistic of female violence.

I remained silent and hidden while removing my motorcycle glove and approaching him from behind.

"Hey, asshole!"

I called as I gathered his attention.

Headbutting him with my helmet was enough to render him disoriented.

Before he could regain himself, I grabbed his neck and dove into his mind. Desperately, I rummaged through his every memory until I found what I needed. When I came back, it was not long before he overpowered me and slammed me against the wall by my neck.

Struggling to breathe, Bell sat on the ground, propped up as she held her chest and bore her coughing. Squinting to see through my visor while fighting off a possible head injury, he attempted to taunt me.

"Lemme guess, another mindless boytoy that this slut has been fucking? Or are you a fag like her homo boyfriend?"

Tightening his grip around my neck, the lights around me began to fade. Though he could not see my eyes, I saw into his.

"You're a good boy Jason. You may not have been the brightest, neither did you listen very often, but you were always a good boy. Do mama one last favour, look after Blakey, you're all he has in this world. Do that one last thing for mama."

In my time of desperation, I quoted to him his mother's dying words, bringing tears to his eyes as I felt his grip waver.

In any other scenario, I would have gotten my ass kicked, but I saw in his memories that his brother was killed by a stray bullet in a drive-by shooting. Not something anyone wants to have to use to their advantage.

He was shattered; brought to pieces long enough for me to wedge my boot between his leg with a swift kick. Releasing his hold, I dropped to the ground as he struggled to stay upright with the pain. His refusal to give up was a bit impressive. Staggering as one of his hands grabbed at his crotch and the other with pointed fingers, he moved towards me. With a grunt and wail as she struggled to swing the iron pipe, Bell managed to knock him out long enough for us to tie him up and call the police.

Taking about fifteen minutes to arrive, when they came, officers took our statements and shoved Jason into the back of their S.U.V.

Strolling in as he was being driven out, Vik dropped his boxes of Chinese food, pushed through the crowd of prying eyes that had gathered, and ran over to us. Apprehended by one of the male officers, they refused to let him in, until I left Bell and walked over. After getting him to calm down, I told him everything that transpired. Pulling me into his arms, he held me tight and spoke a sincere thank you into my ear.

Before I knew it, it was past four in the evening and my cell phone that was stashed in my bookbag, had sixteen missed calls—all from Elli. When I called her back and told her what happened, she insisted we all meet at her apartment and spend the night. Not wanting to leave Bell alone, I agreed and extended to both her and Vik, Elli's invitation. When the officers finally left, and her uncle came back from his trip to the Bamboo for car parts, we gathered Bell's things—Vik took her keys.

When we arrived and made it up the stairs, Elli started crying as she wrapped her arms around Bell. I could tell she was not in a mood to be touched but she endured it because it was Elli. Jumping to me, she squeezed me tightly and blurted out how happy and relieved she was that I was okay. Giving her a kiss, I assured her that I was fine and asked about her last exam.

Truthfully the rest of the night I spent in my head—Bell seemed to do the same. Both Elli and Vik tried to distract us, cheer us up, but nothing could have changed the grim thoughts and, in my case, guilt that pranced freely through my mind. Like an unsupervised child in a toy store, my blackened emotions touched, pushed, and meddled with all efforts I made to think happy thoughts. I knew that despite what I faced in my head at the time, Bell's demons were way worse. All I could do was try to understand how she felt.

Usually, a rough, tough, independent kind of girl, in that situation she was powerless. Completely helpless and at the mercy of that sicko, I could only imagine the immense fear she felt.

What was meant to be a night celebrating the end of our exams, turned into a string of movies and snacks while sitting in silence as we all tried to process everything that had happened. Elli brought the mattress from her bed into the living room—struggling the entire time while insisting that she could manage.

Using the couch cushions, we were all able to sleep relatively close to one another. No one really wanted to leave Bell alone—we all wanted to be near in case she needed anything. By half-past twelve, everyone was asleep except for her. I had just dozed off and began slipping into my dreams.

The raising beep of an E.K.G. grew louder.

Blinded by flashes of bright white and shadowy darkness, I heard an old woman's plea.

"Look after Blakey...you're all he has...look after him Jason," right before she flatlined.

Gripped by a depression I knew was not my own, I was pulled into a sinking pit of sadness and self-loathing. With blood on my clothes and his body in my arms, I cried as I called to the skies—the voice in my dreams ringing past my lips and echoing through the living room, "Blakeyyyyy!!!!"

In a cold sweat, I awoke next to Elli while Vik was wrapped like a Mummy in his blanket on the opposite end of our make-shift bed. Reminding myself that those were not my memories, and the pain was not my pain, did not completely erase how I felt, but it did help to numb the sting. Needing a bit of cold water on my face, I made my way to the washroom, doing my best not to wake Elli or Vik. After fully regaining my composure, and dealing with the emotions, I stepped out only to notice the front door was ajar. After peaking outside and realizing it was Bell who left it open, I joined her and closed the door behind me.

Smoking what looked like her third roll of Mary Jane, her eyes were red and puffy making it easy to tell that she had also been crying.

"Hey...want some company?" I asked even though I already closed the door.

"Yeah, pull up a rail," she murmured as she leaned against the railing, staring up into the sea of black, strewn with twinkling stars. Lost in thought, she spoke as her eyes looked off into the distance.

"Before I could finish school, my mom died. It was just me and my dad… and after her death, all he did was work and drink. I met Jason when I was in high school. He was in form five at the time—two years ahead of me. He was so kind, and sweet and loving…"

Breaking down, she turned to me and buried her face in my chest. Feeling the weight of her sadness, her sobs tugged heavily on my heart. After a sniffle or two, she cleared her nose and continued her story.

"I was blind, I guess. I just had the biggest crush on him…all the girls did. My friend Jane, who could never shut her mouth, told Jason how I felt. It was embarrassing. A bit after lunch, he sent a message with one of his friends, asking me to stay back after school and meet him in the form five classroom. That was the…my first time…and I had stronger feelings for him ever since. I felt like a queen bee. He showed me off to all his friends, and all the girls from both our classes envied me. If only they knew how much of a monster he was. Sadly, I found out a bit too late. My dad had been drinking more than usual. He got into this habit of breaking things and cursing in fits of rage when he got drunk. One time he took it too far and slapped me…I left for Jason's that night and hadn't been back home since. It was great, we did all the things couples in the movies would do, we even started arguing, and once it started it just got worse. I managed to bear with it until I graduated, but when I got accepted at UWI into their pre-degree program and moved into an apartment near campus, he lost it. He constantly accused me of cheating and made me cry time and time again over the phone—it didn't matter where I was or what I was doing. I had to answer cuz' if I didn't it meant I was off being a whore. It wasn't long until our arguments got physical...his words were no longer enough so he had to lay his hands on me whenever we disagreed or I didn't answer when he called, or if I didn't call him right back... I felt like I was a prisoner in my own life, but I was terrified of him. The day Viktor's dad put him out and he came to my apartment, he walked in on me, bleeding. Jason threw an empty stag bottle at me. It barely missed my face and shattered against the wall. A piece flew and cut me right here."

She pointed to the scar over her eye.

"Vik...Vik went crazy...he dropped his things and just rushed at Jason. When he started hitting him, he refused to stop. If I hadn't cried and begged him not to, Vik would have killed him. After that day, he never left my side, and because of him, I was able to escape. Vik gave me my life back—not many are as lucky as I am. Now, whenever I see Jason, I get this feeling...everything stops...my heart starts to pound and I hear the screaming, the yelling, the broken glass. Every time I see him, it terrifies me."

Holding her as she continued to cry, I thought about how she must have felt. Bell, to me, was always this strong-willed, larger-than-life girl who had no cover for her mouth...seeing her cry the way she did fostered within me a new type of sadness.

161

"How could someone treat another human being that way? Torment, accuse, and abuse them until the simple sight of that person paralyzes them with fear. What kind of pathetic man would do that to a woman?"

I contemplated the cruelty of some people.

After all that she told me, one thing stuck out, so I asked.

"Bell…did you want something to happen in that classroom?"

Still buried in my chest, her soft words barely made it to my ears.

"I ask myself that every day."

"I know what that feels like."

I tried to relate to her, hoping in that moment it made her feel less like 'the only one'.

"Miss Alysandra?"

"Yeah, thinking back on it now, I find myself questioning if I had really wanted it. She was just so…"

"Show me."

Still in my embrace, she spoke into my chest as she waited for me to invite her into my head. After the run-in with her ex, Jason, I was in no mood to use my abilities, but I felt as though Bell really wanted to see if I understood—if I truly got the pain she was feeling.

She just wanted someone to relate to, even though the relation was a grim one.

Not saying a thing, I placed my palm on the back of her neck and pulled her into my many memories of Miss Alysandra. I showed her all there was to see. She saw every single time Miss Aly called me in with nothing but a finger and made me eat her pussy. She witnessed all the times she rode my cock on the chairs and tables of the many classrooms we fucked in. She even saw me tonguing Miss Aly's cunt and working her hole with my fingers till she came and me licking her eagerly from my lips while under her desk in the staffroom. Finally ending with the memory of my beloved teacher being stuffed and creampied by her husband in the carpark for our school's sports day.

When I finally broke our connection, the only thing she could say through her heavy breathing was, "Wow."

"Yup, miss Aly was really something else."

"Do you still have feelings for her?"

Her question, after casting me to contemplation for a moment, I answered truthfully.

"Honestly, I think I do… but it's more anger than anything else. I never admitted it to myself at the time, but when those things started to happen between Miss Aly and me, I was genuinely scared. I don't know why but I fought that fear—I shoved it down and convinced myself that I was becoming a man and I wanted it. I was so sure what I had felt towards her back then was love. Being with Elli now makes me wonder how could I have been that naive and blind."

"It's not your fault. When you're young you don't know any better. The things we chase sometimes end up being the worst things for us."

After a while, we both realized that we were still locked in each other's arms. Not letting me go, Bell leaned back and drove her gaze from the depths of my chest to my eyes.

"What the hell was happening!"

Chapter Eighteen

I should have let her go.

There and then I should have unknotted my fingers, opened my arms, and stepped back. But this heat that rose from my chest, getting hotter with each passing breath I took, drove a light-headedness through my skull that kept my fingers woven tightly. I fought every muscle and ounce of being in blissful failure as Bell leaned in and I followed. The moment her soft, cold lips pressed against mine and the smoke on her breath brushed against my nose, I knew...there was no turning back.

What started as a stolen kiss born from sadness, or maybe vulnerability, turned to fiery locked lips and keen tongues that danced and swirled in the slowly rising heat of the moment. In a loose-fitting pair of grey sweatpants and a tight black vest, she pressed her busty chest against me. It obviously felt different from kissing Elli seeing that Bell had two cup sizes over her.

Stealing my hands from her waist, she lured them to the petite cheeks of her little ass. I was once again reminded of the differences between my girlfriend and one of her best friends. Bell's lack of butt did little to deter my wandering fingers. Gripping her cheeks, I felt her tush spread under the force of my hands. Pressed against my body, her bountiful tits climbed to the low-hung neckline of her top, drawing my eyes as we kissed and revelled in our bad decision.

Turning her back to me, she leaned her head and rested it on my shoulder. With the aid of her hand, she pulled me in until our lips met again. Seduced by her kiss and the flicks of her talented tongue, she guided my fingertips along the skin of her flat stomach. Trailing under her vest, she led my icy hands as they explored her smouldering flesh. Cupping one of her magnificent breasts, I fondled her nipples between my fingers as she moaned into our kiss.

Boldly sliding my free hand into her sweatpants, I admired the sultry sensation of her freshly shaven pussy against my fingers and palm. Already wet, I easily slipped between her lips and teased her hole before sliding two fingers into her cunt. The sound that slipped past her lips sent a pulsing wave of lust to my stiffening cock that was joyously wedged between her ass cheeks. Grinding her hips, she refused to break our kiss as she gently stroked my rod to a full erection.

Flowing freely, the juices from her slushing pussy coated my hand and formed a wet stain on the crotch of her pants.

In the heat of it all, something told me to look up. Raising my head just in time, I saw the curtains inside Elli's apartment rustle. The sharp spike of fear that stabbed me was enough to completely kill the mood and plunge me into a guilt-ridden state. Hopping off my arousal, I boarded the train of regret almost instantly.

"Shit…I think someone saw us, Bell."

Pulling my hand out of her pussy, she sighed, "Damn…you sure someone saw?"

"I think so, I saw the curtains moving."

"Crappp…okay look, I know Vik…he'd understand. It was just a moment of weakness."

"Was it really?" I asked, casting doubt upon her face.

"I think so…okay so what if it wasn't? It's not like we had sex right?"

"That's not the point Bell…we're all friends and I love Elli. I don't wanna lose her, I don't wanna lose any of you guys."

"Look it's not that bad okay D. We'd just tell them the truth and hope they forgive us."

167

"Vik might forgive you! You guys do all kinds of wild things. I don't think Elli would be so understanding."

"Look, if we're caught, we're caught. We'd just face it together…okay?"

"Okay," I said as I felt the tug of my reservations.

I did not want to lie, nor did I want to lose Elli. I was less than sure about Bell's plan, but it was the only one we had.

Taking the lead, she opened the door and stepped inside. Still gleaming from her pussy juice, I remembered she was still on my fingers. In an untimely moment of weakness, I rubbed them on my lips and licked her off, enjoying the mild saltiness, just as she turned around and got a glimpse of me tasting her. Refusing to acknowledge it, her widened eyes were enough to signal that she had seen me.

Ready to face the music, I stepped inside only to be met by a sleeping Elli and Vik while the fan spun and blew air against the curtains. Feeling a wave of relief, I was not spared the guilt as Bell and I promised to come clean with them both the next day.

Chapter Nineteen

When the sun rose and dragged the morning with it, Elli turned to find me awake next to her on the mattress. Having endured a sleepless night, my "Good morning, babe" rung a bit shy of enthusiasm as she shimmied over and placed her head of wild, frizzy hair on my chest.

Not wanting to hint that something was wrong, I did my best to do what I always did—stroked her hair, caressed her cheek, and even spanked her jiggly ass as she shuffled off to the washroom. Noticing that Vik and Bell weren't around, I decided to step outside to see if her car was still in the car park. Scaring me half to death when I opened the door, Vik was standing there with his hand out as if he had just reached for the doorknob. Not

169

knowing what to expect because I was still unsure whether he saw or not, I braced for the worst.

"Morning buddy!"

He greeted me by ruffling my hair as he stepped inside.

Walking towards Bell, Vik ventured into the apartment in search of Elli.

"Did he see us? Did he say anything? Would he tell Elli?"

Bombarding Bell with my mirage of questions, her sleepless night made her agitated.

"Firstly…keep your voice down. Secondly, no he didn't say anything. I told you he didn't see us. Would you just relax!"

Cutting us off, Vik popped his head out the door.

"Hey babe, Elli and I are gonna go into Chaguanas so I could pick an anniversary present out for ma, okay? It'll just be you and D for the day, we should get back around three. Oh, and I'm borrowing the car."

Clearly, without a choice in the matter, Bell simply nodded as I felt the dread set into my gut over the fact that she and I were going to be alone in the apartment. Knowing that I could not afford another screwup, I was positive that I would behave myself, but Bell was another story, or so I thought.

When Vik and Elli finally left, to my surprise, Bell insisted that we decorate the apartment with flowers and some candles and make them dinner as a way to apologize. After hearing her solution, I felt stupid for assuming that it would have played out like a cliché porno.

In agreement, we hopped on Gabriella and rode until we found a flower shop. It did not take long since Couva was a few minutes away. We also made a quick stop at the grocery to buy chocolates and ingredients for spaghetti and meatballs.

By the time we got back home, spread the petals, and lit the candles, they had gotten back from their little trip.

Without food because Bell burnt the meatballs and I overcooked the pasta, we ordered pizza that hadn't arrived yet. When I heard Vik turning the knob, I felt as though the floor could have opened up and swallowed me, and it still would have been better than what I had to face.

Surprised, they both took turns roaming the living room, admiring the candles and many strewn petals.

"What's the occasion?"

Glaring at each other, Bell and I had one of those 'it's now or never moments' as I took the lead.

"Guys, we kinda need to tell you both something. We should have a seat."

171

Sitting next to Bell, we faced Elli and Vik on the couch next to us. Wanting to take things slow, I fumbled to find the right words.

"So…urm…It's like this…" Not my best line but to be fair my mind was a mess of chaos, questions, and reservations at the time. "Something happened…"

"Last night Darion came outside and saw me crying. One thing led to another, we kissed and he fingered my pussy. It was a dumb thing to do…we both know that and we're both sorry. Elli, Vik babe, I was just in a bad place. I really am sorry, and I know D is too."

Never being one for subtlety, Bell ripped the bandage off and apologized for us both in the process. Not knowing what I could have really added at that point, I looked both Vik and Elli in the eyes.

"Vik, buddy I really am sorry, and Elli, babe I never meant to hurt you, I really didn't."

Turning to each other they smiled leaving Bell and I beyond lost for words.

"We know…" Elli said, in a rather calm, seemingly cheery voice, "Vik saw the both of you last night. We just wanted to see if you guys would have told us the truth."

After a few moments of silent stares, I could not help myself.

"So, all is forgiven?" I stupidly asked.

Not even the slightest bit angry, they laughed and looked at us both.

"No no no…it's not gonna be that easy. Both of you did a stupid thing, it's only fair that Vik and I punish you guys."

Wanting to torture us a bit, they insisted we wait until Friday to find out what they had come up with. Just three days away, it would give my overactive mind ample time to torture me with made-up scenarios.

"So, what's for dinner!?"

Vik sprang from his seat and strolled over to the kitchen.

Knowing it was only fair that I endure the playful torture, I decided against pestering Elli to tell me what the punishment would be.

"Damn…Bell, were you in the kitchen again?" Vik asked after lifting the lid of the chard frying pan.

"We tried to make you guys dinner, okay. It just…it was the stove's fault anyway. Elli, you need to get that thing fixed."

Sharing a laugh amongst themselves I was stunned to see how they perfectly coexisted despite what we had just admitted to. It changed nothing, they laughed, smiled, and chattered on without a care, inviting me to do the same. I felt privileged at that moment to have such an awe-inspiring group of friends and a girlfriend like Elli.

After about ten minutes, I heard the pizza delivery guy pull up on his motorcycle. Before long, thee knocks played against the door, prompting Elli to rush over. When she swung it open, she stood frozen for a second before it slipped out of her mouth.

"Ella."

"Do I know you?" she asked as Elli fumbled with her words.

"Ella…" I called as I motioned over to her and Elli.

"Darion! …Oh, I see. That's how you knew my name. You had me scared there for a second."

Taking the boxes of pizza from Ella, Elli took them over to the kitchen while we chatted.

"So, how've you been? It's been a while," I asked.

"Well, it's been…a bit… you know, here and there. I got a job delivering pizza—Zatanni said it'll teach me responsibility. Aside from that, it's just lectures and studying…and my bike of course."

"Of course, it's the most important thing."

Giggling as Elli approached with the money.

Turning to her, I could tell she was a bit uneasy and perhaps a bit jealous, but I hadn't seen Ella in so long, I just wanted to catch up a bit.

"Babe, I'm gonna walk Ella down, okay?" I bravely asked.

Less than pleased with my request, her head nodded yes but her face was painted with objections.

Closing the front door behind me, Ella and I spoke as much as we could on our way down.

"How's school been? Managing with classes okay?"

"Yeah, it's great actually, have exams in a while so there's that," she said through partial smiles. "What about you? How's UTT treating you?"

"It's good, I'm learning a lot and I met some amazing people."

"Yeah, I noticed Bell and Viktor, I've seen them around UWI. So…the girl that answered the door, the one that knew my name…is she…"

"My girlfriend? Yeah, her name is Elli, she's really one of a kind."

"That's nice…it's really really nice that you're happy."

Hearing the dips in her voice, I could tell that she was not as okay nor as happy as she claimed to be.

"Well, I have a few more pizzas to deliver. I guess we'd see each other around?"

"I hope so."

She leaned in for a hug before she left. When I took her in my arms, it felt like nothing had changed...there were still jolts of lust and longing between us.

"I miss you sooo much," she murmured under her breath.

Without contention, my heart pushed the truth past my lips.

"I miss you too Ella."

Wanting to seize the chance and look into her mind to see if she was really okay, I settled instead for enjoying our hug until she had to leave. With her tears held back, her pouty lips said it all. Hopping on her bike, she turned the key and rode off until she was nothing more than the sound of a revving engine getting softer with the distance.

When I finally looked up at the apartment, I saw the silhouettes of my friends and girlfriend as they curiously peered through the curtains of the window. Trying to act nonchalant when I got back inside, Vik and Bell pretended to be on their phones while Elli was reading from an upside-down textbook.

"Babe...it's not right side up."

She glanced over the cover without her glasses, while Vik and Bell burst into laughter.

Even though none of them asked, the odd stares and sharp glances over dinner and through our conversations, were more than enough to inform me of their growing curiosities.

After hopping from one trivial topic to the next, Bell had had enough and blurted out her question.

"So what's the deal with that Ella chick? She was your perfect ex biker-girlfriend or something?"

Draping a blanket of silence over the room, I could feel Vik and Elli's anticipation towards my pending answer.

"It's not like that…at least it wasn't like that with me and her. She wasn't really my girlfriend…it's a bit complicated."

Hoping to end the conversation there, Bell was reluctant to give in.

"So it was just a fucking thing?" she asked as I noticed Elli shift in her chair.

By no means was I a genius, but even I could tell that Elli was intimidated by Ella. Opposite in nature and vastly different in physique, their only commonality was their love of motorcycles.

"No, it was more than that…like I said Bell, it's complicated."

"Why don't you show them?" Elli suggested.

Genuinely surprised at her words, all I could manage to do was ask, "What?"

"Yeah, why not just show them? I've already seen your memories of her, plus you've told me more than enough. Why not let Vik and Bell see? They know about your powers, so it won't hurt to share. But only if you're okay with it."

Knowing that I had a lot to make up for after what happened with Bell, I agreed despite my internal protests. I thought the least I could do to show Elli I was sorry, was to say yes to everything that she asked. It was not the brightest idea, but it felt more like I was making amends that way.

Placing my open palms on the table, I invited them both to take hold. With the rush of thoughts and worries that frisked freely through my head, I didn't realize that I was attempting to let two people into my mind at the same time. I did just have a run-in with an old flame and was hanging from the gallows of a bad decision—my mind was understandably in disarray.

Immediately feeling the mental strain, I struggled to show them both the same memories. Taking them back to the first day I met Ella, they saw it was not long before she was teasing me with her heaving breasts, supple ass, and neatly trimmed pussy on the beach. In the change room, they witnessed me stretching her little asshole as her nails clawed at the concrete slab, right before I flooded her ass with cum. They saw us going at it like animals in the back seat of a car in Space's carpark as she smothered my face with her cunt. When I showed them what had happened between Zatanni and me, I started losing control. Against my better efforts, they saw

178

Ella and me that night on the benches in UWI and heard everything she told me. By the time I pushed them both out of my head, they had known her story. A fact that I felt great guilt over, seeing that it was not mine to share.

"Wow, that was something else," Vik said, while Bell remained in silence.

Seeing and hearing what Ella had been through played on her empathy. She was able to relate to Ella in more ways than one and I could tell that rattled around in her head for the rest of the night.

Chapter Twenty

With everyone finding sleep easily, I was left awake. Staring at Vik and Bell cuddled up on the couch next to me, I caressed Elli's legs and feet while I was locked in thought. Because she didn't yell, scream or even get angry when she found out about Bell and me, made me feel more guilt-ridden. She was so quick to understand and forgive me that it made everything feel worse. My guilt felt like it weighed ten times as much.

Driven by my will to make it up to her, I fought through my tiredness until I came up with the perfect plan. Seeing that it was so short notice, there wasn't much I could offer her to show that I was sorry, but I could go all out and give her a mind-blowing experience.

Through My Eyes – The First Five

A bit of a novice when it came to sex, Elli's fetishes always pertained to cosplay. She had never had any over-the-top experiences—I intended to change that. Admittingly, thinking about the things I wanted to do to her, drove the hooks of lust deeper into me. I felt the rising heat—that sprawling sensation that came with arousal.

In my head, it started off as a way to apologize, but now my loins craved her and with every pulse of my growing dick—the want to ravish her body became more seductive. It was like…something flicked on—as if a switch flipped and my thoughts were about all the ways that I could use her holes to please myself.

Following the allure of what I desired, I gently lifted her legs off my lap and tiptoed to her bedroom. Dawning her favorite headband, I stripped off my clothes before shuffling through her wardroom until I found the red and yellow novelty tie that went with her wizard costume. Once everything I needed was easily accessible, I strolled into the living room wearing nothing but my birthday suit. Opting to not nudge her awake, I knelt beside the couch and kissed her until her eyes opened and her lips followed my lead.

Leaning in, I whispered in her ear as she fiddled to find her glasses.

"Come to the bedroom kitten."

Giving her a view of my bare ass as I walked off, I slipped into the room and stood behind the door.

"Babe?" she called out as she stepped in.

I pushed the door close—the click of its lock spun her around to face me.

With nothing on but her ninja headband, her eyebrows hoisted at their arches as her eyes widened and her freckles vanished into her reddening cheeks. Before she could utter another word, I stepped towards her, locking eyes until I took her chin between my fingers.

"I want you...so I'm going to take you."

I whispered to her as my encroaching lips rendered whatever doubts or opinions she had, mute.

The moment we kissed was the point I truly lost all control. Elli and I had kissed so many times before, but it never made me feel like this.

Was it because of my guilt?

It was more than just desire...more than just this smouldering flame. I wanted to fuck her until her legs quivered...until her orgasms became too much to bear. I yearned to stuff my cock into her cunt as deep as it could go and pound away at her flesh. I wanted to make her scream my name—she needed to scream my name. I needed to hear her beg me to stop.

These were urges that, before tonight, I never knew I had, and they easily bent my will and influenced my cravings. I fell prey to their desires, and she was about to fall prey to mine.

With our lips locked, I grew angry at her clothes for being in the way. I was genuinely irritated that I could not feel the sensation of her bare skin against mine. Hooking the straps of her top, I only intended to pull them off until I heard the ripping of fabric. Tearing her top off her shoulders, her petite breasts refused to pop out—instead, they just hung there in all their A-cupped glory.

Pointed, her dark brown nipples stood proudly on her chest. I licked my lips while I explored her body with my eyes. With her torn top falling to the floor, I guided my fingers to the back of her head and wove them between a handful of her frizzy hair. Locking them tightly, I yanked her head back, causing her to let out a soft whimper. Dragging my tongue along her neck, I traced up to her jaw before moving to the bottom of her chin and then to her lips. I wanted her to feel my longing through my kiss…to know exactly how sorry I was and how much I simply craved her.

Biting her lips, I nibbled on her tongue before turning her around and pushing her. As she fell forward, she placed her hands on the mattress and was bent over at the edge of the bed.

"Good, now stay there like a good little whore."

I cupped the freckled cheeks of her bountiful ass, squeezing them as her flesh sunk between my fingers. With a swing of my palm, the sound of her spanking echoed through the bedroom as she jerked forward casting a soft moan. With two more slaps of my palm, the freckles on her butt blended into the cherry red of her tender skin. When I dropped to my knees, I stuck my face between the cheeks of her ass and immediately dug my tongue into her pussy. Not yet wet, I worked her until her juices were smeared all over my lips and nose. Her smell and taste were like dangerous catalysts, reacting with my already insatiable concoction of want, need, and desire. I lost myself in the sounds that escaped her lips, the taste of her dribbling slit, and the feeling of her soft fleshy clit against my tongue.

The more I sucked her clit and stole sips of her juices, the more her legs trembled as she clawed at the sheets.

"Babe...I think I'm gonna cum!" Her cunt got wetter as she took to the tips of her toes, riding the building wave of her orgasm.

"Babbeeeee...I'm gonnnaa cummmm!"

Just before the wave came crashing over her, I stopped, stood up, and looked on as her body faintly spasmed.

"Climb on the bed and sit."

"What?" she asked through heavy breaths.

Knowing that she heard me, I slapped the already red cheeks of her ass so hard that she cried out.

"Ouch babe! That hurt!"

184

So, I did it again, forcing her to grab her cheek and turn to meet my gaze. Unphased that I had hurt her, I demanded her compliance.

"Climb onto the bed and sit you little slut! Oh, and I didn't say you could speak."

In her eyes, I saw the very moment all her uncertainties melted away. Like putty, her desire to be taken drove her to obey me. In silence, she climbed onto the bed, making sure to give me a clear view of her ass and glistening lips as she crawled. When she finally sat at the centre of the mattress, she hugged her knees against her chest and patiently waited, staring at me.

I felt like there was no love in my eyes. Looking at her, naked on the bed, I no longer saw my girlfriend. Instead, she was like a fix—her body was my drug of choice and I intended to use and abuse it until it quelled the raging fire in my loins.

Fishing through her nightstand, I pulled out her tiny bottle of lube and purple dildo. As she opened her mouth to protest in embarrassment, I cleared my throat and rendered her silent.

"Whores don't speak! They look, they listen, and they obey!"

Tossing her toy onto the bed, I snapped open the bottle and dripped a few drops of lube onto my stiff cock. Making my way to the end of the room, I pulled her desk chair and positioned it in front of her bed. When I sat, I stroked my rod until it glistened. Completely covered in lube, I worked the head of my dick between my fingers before teasing the length of my shaft.

"Play."

I glanced at her and then at the toy on the bed.

Timidly picking it up, she looked at it and then at me. I could tell she was nervous—maybe a bit self-conscious. I didn't care. It didn't matter to me how she thought she looked when she played with herself—I knew for a fact she looked exquisitely sexy and erotic.

Taking a bit too long, I instructed her once more.

"Stick it in your mouth and suck it like a cock."

Without question, she brought it to her mouth and ran it between her lips as she licked it with her flicking tongue.

"Good. Now lean back and spread your legs…Wider. That's it, show daddy your pussy. Good girl. Now turn it on and hold it against your clit."

Hearing her dildo hum to life, she slid it over her mound and onto her tiny jewel. Moving it in small circles, her legs began pulling in bit by bit.

"How does it feel?"

Barely able to get her words out, all she could utter was a breathy, "Amazing."

"Show me how you fuck yourself, pretty slut."

Effortlessly sliding the toy into her cunt, she leaned into the pillows behind her. Cupping her tits with her free hand, she pinched at her nipples until they were proudly pointed. Moaning as she fucked herself, I stared at her the entire time, and she stared back. I saw her nibble at her bottom lip, her stretching and curling toes, and the juices flowing freely from her snatch. I saw her roll her nipples and tug at the bedsheets as she once again got close to her orgasm. With her moans climbing, I got out of my chair and hastily strutted over to the bed. Grabbing her wrist as she furiously toyed her spilling hole, I stopped her right at the edge, right before she dove into orgasmic bliss. Sliding it out of her, the purple plastic gleamed with her honey. Taking it from her hands, I turned it off and brought it to my lips. Exploring it with my tongue, I licked every drop of her off her dildo.

"Give me your hands."

Reaching for her novelty tie, I bound her wrists and fastened them to the head of the bed. Kneeling on the mattress, I hooked her legs over my shoulders and positioned my rod. Being gentle was the last thing on my mind—this was not making love. No, this was fucking.

In a single stroke, I rammed every inch of me into her. Tugging at her bindings, she gasped as her entire hole was stuffed. I leaned forward and thrusted my hips—a bit gentle for about three seconds before it grew to a relentless pounding as Elli was no longer able to muffle her sounds of eroticism.

"Fuck…this pussy feels good!" I proclaimed between breaths.

Lifting her legs, I pushed them back and held them open. Now her legs were as wide as they could spread, giving us both a clear view of my cock eagerly and furiously slipping in and out of her cunt. The sultry sounds of thumping flesh got louder, symphonizing with her resounding moans and the rhythm of her rocking bed.

"Hokage…I'm gonna cum…Mmmmm. Fuck I'm cumminggggg!"

"Yes, that's it…cum for me you little slut. Cum on my cock!"

Gripped by the walls of her pussy, she pushed me out of her hole as she gushed and squirted, showering me with her ejaculation. Like a child in the rain, I stuck my tongue out hoping that some of her landed on my lips before I dove between her legs to get a better taste.

"Mmmmm"

Her mild sweetness slid to the back of my throat.

"Between your legs is my favorite place to eat. I love that you taste so good baby. Now bend over and show me that ass."

Fumbling to turn around with her hands tied, she finally managed. Placing her face on a pillow, she arched her back, proudly displaying her voluptuous ass and gaping hole. Cramming her full of my dick, I gripped her waist and pulled her into me. With each slap of bare skin, a shallow grunt jumped beyond her lips. Leaning in, I pressed her head down and drove my rod into her slippery hole. With each thrust, her cheeks rippled giving me glances of her peeking asshole.

I stopped and slid out of her, bringing my face to her ass. I spread her cheeks and spat on her little hole. Shoving myself back into her pussy, I circled her freshly lubed backdoor with my thumb. With each stroke into her cunt, I worked my thumb bit by bit until it slid into her ass. Seemingly pulling me in, soon my thumb was buried deep in her butt, all the way to its final joint. She came again and again until her bed was soaked, and her orgasm traipsed along the fine line of pain and pleasure.

Finally feeling the rise of my climax, my thrusts grew wild and erratic as my legs felt that delightful weakness. Pulling my cock out, I cast my last demand.

"Spread your ass for daddy!"

Like a good little slut, she complied and parted her cheeks so that I could spurt streams of thick cum onto her asshole. Spent, I was hypnotized by the way the milky white ropes trailed down her crack, dripped off her clit and pooled onto the bedsheet.

Removing her bonds, I laid next to her as I revelled in the aftershocks of my orgasm. As it faded, I felt a small bit of guilt over spanking her so hard and tearing her top. Whatever it was that had come over me was satisfied and no longer meddled with my desires.

"Is your butt okay?" I asked being guided by my fresh guilt.

"It hurts a bit, but wow was it worth it." She said as newfound energy riddled her voice.

"Could I kiss it, so that it feels better?" I asked knowing that no medical evidence has ever proven such a thing.

"Sure, just be gentle okay."

Turning over, she showed me her bright red cheeks that were embellished with my handprints. Gently I kissed them as I caressed her bruised skin with the tips of my fingers.

After a while, I worked her into my arms, told her that I was sorry, and I loved her before we both drifted to sleep.

Chapter Twenty-one

When morning came and I finally woke up, Elli and Vik had already gone to buy Doubles leaving Bell and me behind. Wiping the sleep from my eyes, I groggily made my way to the bathroom. Opening the door, there she was.

"Someone had fun last night!" she mocked.

"Sorry Bell, I didn't know you were in here."

I tried not to look at her blue, laced panties or her perky tits through her vest.

"It's okay D. You could come in—I don't mind sharing. Plus, it's not like you haven't seen me naked before. Compared to that, what I have on now is way more decent."

She plopped a blob of toothpaste onto her toothbrush.

I would not have taken her up on her offer, but I badly need to pee.

Turning my back to her, I whipped it out and did my best to fight 'the shivers'. After two shakes, I joined her at the sink.

It did feel a bit weird being around Bell, but because she never took anything too seriously, my discomfort faded and she and I were back to laughing and chatting like normal. Pulling a pair of chairs up to the kitchen counter, we sat and waited for Vik and Elli to get back with breakfast.

"Hey D. Could I ask you something?"

Her shift in tone made me realize that her question was not going to be one I could easily brush off.

"Sure…What's on your mind?"

"The other night…when we…you know. What woke you up? I swore I heard you scream something before you came outside."

With a sigh, I answered her question.

"When I use my powers and look into people's minds, I'm able to see anything and everything. It sounds fun… but there are some dark things locked away in people's heads. When I witness their worst memories, it leaves an impression. Once I see it, I experience it, and with bad memories, I often feel it. I feel the person's pain... their guilt and sadness... it haunts my dreams. When I wake up, I have to do everything I can to convince myself the pain I'm feeling is not mine."

"So, with Jason?"

"Yeah, I touched him while we fought and used his memories against him," I said as the look on her face changed.

"Why would you put yourself through that?"

"What do you mean why? Bell, you mean the world to Elli, she loves you and Vik dearly, and honestly, so do I. I love all three of you guys and I'd never stand by and see any of you get hurt. A couple nightmares and bad feelings won't compare to the pain I'd feel if I lost one of you."

Before she could respond, Vik and Elli walked through the door, each with a small, brown, paper bag in their hands. Almost immediately the mouth-watering smell of Doubles flooded the entire apartment.

"Time to eat!" Vik hollered.

We all dug into the bags and finished our wrapped pieces of culinary heaven.

With very few words spoken through chews, after breakfast the four of us just sat around the apartment.

Bell and Vik studied for their upcoming exams, while Elli and I tidied up.

It was a day filled mostly with relaxation.

Once the chores were done, Elli and I spent the rest of the day in bed. Yes, we did indulge in some light foreplay, but our conversation is what drove time hastily past us. I enjoyed times like these. Yeah…sex was great and all, but really getting to know Elli is what made it even better. Amidst the array of topics, I fell prey to the urge to ask.

"Babe… about my punishment…"

"Eh!... Nope, I'm not going to tell you. You'd just have to wait until Friday, like Bell."

Respecting her wishes and teasing, I counted the hours until Friday day came, and what a great twenty-nine hours, fifty-four minutes, and twenty-seven seconds they were for my overactive imagination.

When Friday dawned, nothing happened out of the ordinary. Elli and I were in her apartment—we ate, watched a couple of movies, and enjoyed the fact that our exams and the semester were over. Vik and Bell on the other hand were attending their first exam, but still made it known that we had to hang out that evening.

Deciding to give The Rise a little break and try someplace new, we went exploring. Initially stopping at Atlantic Plaza to get some food, we stumbled across a small restaurant and bar that had now opened called Mini

Bar. The name explained it perfectly—it was definitely a 'mini bar', but it was beautiful on the inside. It was infrastructure's version of 'don't judge a book by its cover' or in this case, the front door.

With a bar that sprawled the length of the room, it was like an oversized toothpaste box with the washrooms at the end. Most of the employees with the exception of the bouncer and manager were Latinas. It quickly became our favorite spot. The beers were always ice cold, the music was always loud and trendy, and the bartenders and waitresses were always pleasant and friendly. You would think it was their job, but a handful of them knew us by name and always stayed a bit too long chatting with us whenever we came in.

Seeing that this was our first time here, we tried some of their signature shots and drinks. Bell loved the blowjob shot and drank it how it was meant to be drank. Elli who was practically forced by Bell to do her first-ever shot, had trouble holding the rim of the glass with her lips, so she opted to drink it like a normal person.

We had so much fun, we did not care that there was no dancing.

After rounds of drinks and shots, Vik peered at his watch before whispering into Elli's ear.

"Okay time to go," she said after hearing what Vik had to say.

"Wait, what? Whyyyyyy?" Bell whined.

"Punishment time!"

She teased us.

With her apartment less than a few minutes away, the ride there somehow felt like an eternity. With the tipsiness lingering in my system, I felt an odd mix of anxiety and questionable anticipation. Bell nor I had any idea what we were in store for, but according to Bell, knowing Vik, it would be something exciting. I was not so thrilled—my mind refusing to let go of my anxiety, prompted me to believe that I did not drink enough in the first place.

When we parked and walked up the staircase to the front door, Elli and Vik made Bell and I wait outside. We heard a bit of rummaging for a few minutes before Elli's voice rung from deep within the apartment.

"Okay, you guys could come now."

When we walked in, the first thing I noticed was the missing couch from the living room.

"Come into the bedroom," Vik instructed.

"See, I told you it'll be fun."

Bell's face seemed to light up.

I was fully consumed by my anxiety at that moment. I was not too thrilled that my punishment involved the bedroom seeing that Vik was a bit 'bigger' than I was.

"Sit."

Elli pointed to the couch facing the bed as we stepped into the bedroom.

Chapter Twenty-two

Taking our seats, I noticed she was in a fitted top and extremely short shorts. Her magnificent cheeks were clearly visible as the shorts failed to provide any kind of coverage. Vik was almost naked. In only his boxers, his meaty cock fought against its fabric as it bulged proudly.

"So this is what is going to happen…" Elli said with a sense of confidence "…both Bell and you did a stupid thing. Now, you're both going to watch us do the exact same thing."

I felt the green flames of jealousy spread through my chest, but it did not burn alone. In fact, as jealous as I felt, I wanted to watch. With the flames of desire and jealously ravaging me, I chose to sit in silence and just look on.

Taking the back of his head, Elli pulled Vik down to meet her lips. I did feel a sharp stab when their lips touched—after all, those were the lips I loved kissing, yet seeing her work those lips against another man's was seductively sexy.

As they explored each other's bodies, their wandering hands pushed moans past their lips. Hearing Elli sent jolts through my body while my cock pulsed and inched towards a full erection. Bell was enjoying the show. Clearly, without the conflicting views that plagued me, she slipped her hand under the waist of her jeans and played with her pussy. I was turned on, yet the lingering shards of jealously prevented me from taking a page from Bell's book.

Not sure if it was intentional or not, but when Vik spun Elli around and nuzzled his stiff rod between her cheeks, he moaned.

"Damn."

It was obvious that compared to Bell's petite ass, Elli's was thick and glorious. This made her jealous—I could tell because the movement through her jeans stopped instantly. I watched as Vik slid his hand between her breasts, then along her stomach before finally working it into her shorts. Waiting for his fingers to touch her pussy, I felt envious as he made her moan and her legs shyly quivered.

Oddly Elli's eyes often turned to Bell—it became clear that whatever qualms she had, was not so much with me, but with her. Vik on the other hand happily enjoyed the experience—having already forgiven Bell and me, he was more of an assistant during it all.

Bell quickly realized that Elli intended to make her jealous, but when Bell got jealous, she often sought to get even.

Taking to her feet, she glared at Elli as they exchanged stares. Viewing it as an invitation, Elli pushed her ass back and, grinding into Vik's cock, hoisting her eyebrow at Bell before sticking her tongue in his mouth. I heard her breath rush past her flared nostrils and saw her teeth grind as her jaw flexed. I assumed that she finally felt the punishment aspect of it all and maybe she did, but she chose to handle it in her own little way.

She unbuttoned her jeans and slid them to her ankles before smiling at Elli and kicking them aside on the floor. Her little cheeks swallowed the pink of her thongs, while the light of the room gleamed off her smooth skinny legs. She and Elli never broke eye contact—even as she pushed me to lay down on the couch and tossed one of her legs over my face, they intensely stared at each other. Like the slutiest game of chess ever played, each girl made their move, urging one another on as they taunted using our moans of pleasure and willingness to indulge in their heated game.

Looking up at the puffy lips and wet slit of Bell's pussy, she held her thongs to the side as she lowered herself onto my face, moaning and biting her lips sensually as she taunted Elli. Unsure about having Bell's pussy in my mouth, I half-assed my tongue action while peeking at Elli from the corner of my eyes. I was a little less than willing until I saw Elli drop her shorts, turn to Vik and take to her knees. Stroking him through his boxers, Vik was not shy in voicing his moans.

When she pulled it out and I heard her gasp before she started sucking him, I knew it was now all in fair game. No longer hindered by my jealousy, it was now about besting the other team. Vik's cock was bigger than mine—there was no denying that, so I had to pull out all the stops if we were going to win… whatever this was. Luckily, I relished eating pussy, and Bell's tasted and smelt delightful.

I took hold of her waist and pulled her down, digging my tongue past her wet lips and into her hole.

"Oh dear God!"

Her words dancing with her moans as I tongue fucked her cunt.

Elli knew I was good at eating pussy—it always ended with her cumming in my mouth even before we have sex. The thing is, she never had anyone before me, so she had nothing to compare it to, but now, after hearing Bell in her sultry bliss as I worked her with my tongue, she knew that it meant I was damn good. After all, even Bell was impressed.

"Squeeze my tits!" Bell demanded as she rode my face and her juices trickled in long lines off my chin and down my neck. She was dripping and spasming against my prodding tongue.

"Pinch my nipples and make me cum…uhhh… hmmmm…. then I'd let you fuck my tits."

I could tell she was fuming after Bell's last comment. Lacking the bosom Bell had, she wasn't equipped well enough to feel my cock erupt between her tits. After hearing her, Elli's sucking got faster and noticeably sloppier, pulling Vik into ecstasy. I'm not sure if they were that much in sync as a couple but they both made their confession, almost in unison.

"I'm cumming."

Followed by deep grunts, Vik shot his streams of cum into my girlfriend's throat. Grinding harder into my face, Bell worked her clit against my flicking tongue as she peaked, squirted, and nearly drowned me in her orgasm.

Expecting Bell to take it to the next level, I was shocked when Elli demanded that Vik fuck her. In the fading grips of her climax, Bell got off my face and stomped over to Elli. Stepping back, she bumped into her nightstand and fell butt first onto it. Slapping her hands against the wall at either side of Elli's face, Bell looked piercingly into her eyes. Now sitting on her nightstand, with her head and back against the wall, Bell leaned in and kissed her. Grabbing a handful of her frizzy hair, she bit Elli's lips and neck before licking and sucking on her stiff nipples.

Bell whispered to Elli causing her to turn to putty.

"No, I'd fuck you."

Dropping to her knees, Bell stared directly at Elli's pussy perched between her spread legs, at the edge of the nightstand. Burying her face in her slit, her tongue swiftly pushed soft moans beyond Elli's lips. Taking the back of Bell's head, I saw my girlfriend enjoy having her pussy licked and devoured by another woman.

I was so engrossed in the unfolding scene, I forgot that Vik was in the room until he walked over to me. I had no idea what to expect but I felt myself unwillingly dive into a sea of nervousness. Part of me wanted to get up and run, but part wanted to stay and was curious as to what he was about to do to me.

With each step he took, I remembered what I saw the night of his birthday—the way he fucked his guy friend until he was nothing more than a quivering orgasm curled up on the sheets. It made me feel an odd sensation that had my cock throbbing. Standing over me at first, he looked at me with eyes that were brimming with lust. He knelt and unbuckled my belt before removing my jeans and boxer shorts. Sitting up, I instinctively lifted my hips to allow him, while I screamed in my head, "What are you doing!?"

Elli was too busy smearing Bell's face with her pussy to even notice that Vik was now staring at my bare, stiff cock. I could feel my heart pounding away at the inside of my chest as he licked his lips and prepared to take me into his mouth. I had no idea what to expect—with bated breath, it felt like time stood still until his warm and friendly tongue made me moan. Clamping my palm across my lips, I felt a bit of shame knowing that a man made me feel so good.

Vik sucked and stroked my cock better than any woman ever did. As a man, he really did know what men liked, sending waves of pleasure through my entire body. Watching Elli and Bell added to the fire that he had burning between my legs.

Helping her off the nightstand, Bell guided Elli to the bed and made her lie on her back. Positioning herself over Elli's face, Bell was facing Vik and me as our eyes locked, Leaning forward, she stuck her tongue into my girlfriend's drooling cunt. In a glorious display of the sixty-nine position, they both licked, tongued, and slurped each other's juices as their moans were muffled by the soft flesh of the clits between their lips.

The click of an opening lube bottle quickly broke my trance and drew my attention to Vik. With my cock still in his mouth, he dropped a healthy slathering onto his index finger.

"He's going to finger me!"

I contested my reservations with my growing curiosity.

Through My Eyes – The First Five

I took so long deciding if to voice my protest that my words slipped out as a whimper when I felt the pressure of his finger prodding my tight hole. Wincing as it entered me, he slid it to the first knuckle before holding it in place and swirling his tongue around the head of my cock. The pleasure of his mouth rivalled and defeated the pain, allowing him to slide all the way in.

It felt amazing as his fingers fiddled a bit before finding my spot. I didn't know what it was at the time—all I knew was that it drove jolts of foreign pleasure along the shaft of my cock, and I loved how it felt. Teasing me, he massaged that spot until I felt my precum dribble into his mouth before he stopped and started moving his finger back and forth. Fingering me, he made the most feminine whimpers hang on my breath. With my toes curling, each pulse of my cock between his lips caused my hole to tighten on his finger as he slid it in and out of my ass.

Pulling out, I heard the bottle of lube click open yet again. This time he poured it all over two of his fingers, before lining them up with my asshole.

"You ready?"

I nodded yes as my mind was completely void of doubt and occupied to capacity by my desire and curiosity. Feeling the pressure of his fingers, I did my best to let him in as he proceeded to stretch my hole.

"Fuck…" I moaned as I was no longer ashamed of the pleasure I was feeling at the hands of Vik. I felt my hole getting wider as his fingers slid back and forth, while all my pain was quelled by his lips and magic tongue. Right as I was about to give in and let my orgasm overcome me, he stopped and commanded, "Get on the bed."

It had been a while, but I felt the same tug I did back when Miss Aly used to have her way with me. I felt the need to obey, even though the commands came from a man—so I did. I took to my feet, only to fight my shaky legs as I inched over to the bed.

"Climb over Elli and get into the sixty-nine position."

Vik said as Bell hopped off the bed. Skipping over to the nightstand, she opened the drawer and pulled out Elli's purple dildo. Bent over as I loomed over Elli, Bell got between her legs, mere inches from my face.

"Suck this."

She pushed the dildo past my lips. Sticking it to the back of my throat as I gaged, she pulled it out and lowered it to Elli's hole.

"Good, now lick her clit while I fuck her pussy."

Enthusiastically following Bell's instructions, I was too preoccupied licking Elli's tiny jewel and sucking her off the dildo every time Bell pulled it from between her slit, I did not notice Vik sliding a condom onto his thick, meaty staff. When he climbed onto the bed, he positioned himself behind me and took hold of my waist, lowering me and making me arch my back.

"Suck on his cock."

He instructed Elli, who was busy having her pussy toyed.

Feeling her mouth engulf me made it even more sultry knowing that I was about to get fucked. The moment of truth—I felt his latex cladded head poke at my asshole. Already widened from his fingers, his head slid in easily. Gently pushing his hips, the extra lube he applied after putting on the condom, helped him inch into me as I felt my hole getting stretched and stuffed. I felt the pressure of his huge cock as it opened my hole. Baring with the pain, it soon faded to an indescribable sensation that happily dribbled out of my cock. With Bell staring at my face as she fucked Elli with the vibration on, she saw the pain and pleasure her boyfriend was inflicting on my ass, and she loved every second of it.

When Vik finally buried all of his dick into me, he pressed his hips into my spread cheeks, causing my toes to stretch and then finally curl as he slid out. With long strokes, it took a couple of minutes to adjust to the new feeling, but with Elli's lips on my cock as she sucked and it spilled precum, the pain turned to unrivalled pleasure. Long and deep strokes turned to rhythmic slapping that grew to a furious pounding. I could not believe that my ass was withstanding Vik's onslaught and felt amazing doing so. With each thrust of his hips into me, my building orgasm was taken to new heights. My legs were

Dimitri Valentene

trembling, I was moaning, grunting, and calling his name while my precum flowed freely into Elli's throat. It was beyond any kind of pleasure that I had ever felt before…and it was at the hands of a man.

As Vik continued to fuck me while Elli's moans were choked on my cock, Bell took turns fucking her pussy and my mouth with her shimmering purple toy. Still sucking Elli's clit, I enjoyed the pleasures of its sweet, supple flesh against my tongue and between my lips. With her legs coming closer and closer together and her curling toes, Bell knew she was about to cum so she toyed her cunt furiously.

Following his woman, Vik's pounding into my asshole intensified as a building pressure made me claw at the bedsheets. Unable to take it anymore, I felt my cum race along my shaft and spurt into Elli's mouth. My spasming hole gripped Vik's cock as a warmth flooded my ass. Sticking his rod as deep as it could go, I felt its twitch that followed each of his grunts and he came. Elli's moans had risen as she cried out from her climax.

"Fuck…Bellllll…I'm cuminggggggg…"

Squirting like she always does, Bell was taken by surprise after being showered, but I did not fail to jump at the opportunity to taste her, burying my face into her orgasming pussy.

It was over. What had started as a punishment grew into something erotically astounding leaving the four of us spent and perfectly happy as our naked bodies fell onto the bed. Trying to catch her breath, Elli asked, "So…how is it, everyone knows where I keep my dildo?"

Looking at each other, we laughed simply enjoying the moment.

Chapter Twenty-three

All was finally forgiven and with Elli in my arms and Bell in Vik's, Vik and I were cosey and comfortable cuddled up next to each other. I had no regrets at that moment, and I was perfectly happy having learned a lot about myself during that mind-blowing experience. I wasn't jumping ship or anything—I was still very much in love with Elli, but I guess I was more like Vik than I had initially realized.

When silence eventually came to the room, we heard a phone vibrating on the floor. Realizing it was mine, I wondered who was calling at past twelve in the night. Seeing that I had three missed calls, the number seemed familiar, but it had no caller I.D. My phone had definitely seen better days, having to reset it a number of times throughout its life, I frequently lost my contacts.

"Hello?" I answered as I brought it to my ear.

"Hey, Darion… it's Zatanni."

"Hey, Z, what's up? It's been a while. How have you been?"

"Not so good man. She's gone…she killed herself this evening."

Dimitri Valentene

Through My Eyes – The First Five

This book would not have been possible without the support of my friends and family. A special, heartfelt thank you to my Editor and Cover Designer Mc Kayla D. for her support, guidance, and motivation during the writing process. Thank you to Ashley, Christina, Krysten, Kosi, and Karissa for their insights and helpful inputs that made this story what it was.

Excerpt From Book Two

I sat amongst the pews that cradled the many crying faces as all watery eyes were locked onto the casket at the front of the Church. I said less than four words since Zatanni told me. When the words echoed over the line, I couldn't find the strength to grip my phone as it fell to the floor. When Bell, Vik, and Elli asked what was wrong, all I could say was, "Ella's gone."

Sitting in that church, I tried to convince myself that it was real—that in that box was someone I loved dearly that I was never getting to see again. I could not bring myself to do it being brought to tears at the thought of never seeing her again, hearing her laugh, or even hugging her again. I feared the day I lost someone dear to me—now I was living that fear…and a piece of my heart sat in that box.

I did not whimper, wail, or scream. Instead, my tears freely ran from my eyes as I thought to myself.

"I should have looked into her mind that night. I could have done something. I could have changed this."

But it was a bit too late.

She had overdosed on sleeping pills and by the time Zatanni found her, she was already dead. When the time came for people to speak, I did my best to drag myself to the podium.

Reaching into the pocket of my jacket, I pulled out a folded-up sheet of tear-stained paper. On it was the first and last speech I had ever written.

"On days like this, it's hard to find the right words to say, but things like that never stopped Ella. She spoke her mind and at times bore her heart—her words were never laced with lies. She was honest to a fault, sweet and kind—this world did not deserve her. For a long time, I was unhappy, but the day I met her changed all of that. She brought a light into my life that I never thought was possible. Right now, it seems like there's nothing I could do to keep that light burning. With her gone, the world feels different. It feels like it lost more than just a person. I know that today, I've lost more than just a person—that's a piece of my heart in that casket."

Breaking down, my head fell into my bent elbow as I whispered loud enough for the mic to pick up my voice.

"I would do anything to bring you back."

When I finally regained my composure, I approached her to pay my final respects. I don't know why I did it, or what I expected, but I touched her one last time just to see…anything, but it was empty and cold. I knew then she was really gone.

When the service was over and they were leaving to go to the cremation site, I got a moment to speak to Zatanni. Unsure why she did it and still in a mess, all he could have told me about was the fight she and him had when their uncle had to move in with them. When he told me that, all the pieces finally fit together. That day, I let Zatanni know what Ella had been through. Though it was in poor timing, he had to know about the monster he had let into their house.

With all the pieces of the puzzle, I was sure that if I had looked into her mind that night, I would have been able to save her.

Asking Zatanni for a picture of her before I left, he pulled one out of his wallet and handed it to me. Taking him in my arms, I whispered, "I'm really sorry buddy, she meant the world to me too," as I fought back my tears.

Hopping on my bike, I rode off in the opposite direction, not wanting to witness the cremation. Instead, I went to the tattoo shop my dad and I visited when I got accepted into UTT. Handing the artist the picture I had gotten from Zatanni, I told her to fill in the angel's blank face on my arm with Ella's—that way I knew the angel looking after me.

Though after getting inked, it was ill-advised to drink, I gave zero fucks. In my sadness, I rode Gabriella to The Rise, running from my misery as I darted through the cars along the highway.

Did I want to die? Honestly, I'm still unsure, but if I had lost my life that night, I would not have been bothered.

When I finally got to the bar, it was mostly empty seeing that it was around six in the evening on a Monday. When I sat down, I ordered a rum and coke, then another and another, until I was five cups in and drowning my sorrows. It stopped the tears, but did little for the pain, did little to change the fact that she was gone. I blamed myself, and my soul longed to have her back, just to hear her laugh again, just so I could hold her...one last time. At that point in my life, the world never seemed crueller.

As I stared at the melting ice in my glass, I cared very little for the person that left the entire, practically empty, club to sit next to me.

"How've you been, Mr. Valentine?"

Her voice pierced my ears and stabbed my already wounded heart as it sounded a bit too familiar.

217

Dimitri Valentene

"Miss Alysandra…"

COMING JULY 2022

Printed in Great Britain
by Amazon